Elite: Nemorensis

Elite: Nemorensis

SIMON SPURRIER

GOLLANCZ

LONDON

Elite: Dangerous universe, including without limitation plot
and characters, © 2013, 2014 Frontier Developments plc.
All rights reserved.

'ELITE' and the Elite and Frontier logos and Elite: Dangerous
are registered trademarks of Frontier Developments plc.
All rights reserved.

The right of Simon Spurrier to be identified
as the author of this work has been asserted
by him in accordance with the Copyright,
Designs and Patents Act 1988.

First published in Great Britain in 2014 by Gollancz
An imprint of the Orion Publishing Group
Orion House, 5 Upper St Martin's Lane,
London WC2H 9EA
An Hachette UK Company

A CIP catalogue record for this book
is available from the British Library.

ISBN (Cased) 978 1 4732 0126 2

1 3 5 7 9 10 8 6 4 2

Typeset by GroupFMG within BookCloud

Printed in Great Britain by Clays Ltd, St Ives plc

The Orion Publishing Group's policy is to use papers
that are natural, renewable and recyclable products and
made from wood grown in sustainable forests. The logging
and manufacturing processes are expected to conform to
the environmental regulations of the country of origin.

www.simonspurrier.co.uk
www.orionbooks.co.uk
www.gollancz.co.uk

One

Outside, pitching arse over nose, the freighter they'd murdered scattered its guts and prolapsed its crew. Shat its atmosphere with hideous grace and an undeniably romantic sparkle.

And so:

She laughed her breathless laugh. She groaned her mannish groan. She rolled her eyes and repositioned her legs, a lizardlike yank, a feral smile, to pull him deeper inside.

'Myquel,' she whispered, gripping him. 'Myquel Dobroba Pela-LeSire LeQuire.'

It had become her habit, he'd noticed, to murmur his name at least once during sex. Just as it had become his to wonder, when she said it, if she were adoringly savouring the syllables or mocking the pomposity of his having so many. Whichever it was (and with Teesa there was a good chance it was both) the neurotic uncertainty was always banished within moments. Her next movement, her next shudder, her next moan. There simply wasn't room in his brain, he'd accepted, for both her *and* rational thought.

'We should rabbit,' he mumbled, clinging feebly to common sense. 'Right? Snag the goodies and go.'

She ignored it. Another flex of her legs. A groan. A re-anchoring of her hips. He'd known she would.

Myq's ex-career as an intersystemic music icon, and hence as an object of allgender desire, had been admittedly brief. But even in that short time he'd learned a thing or two about gravity-free fucking, and foremost was that one or both participants must have strong legs. That was especially true in the cramped cab of the *Shattergeist*, where every conveniently-positioned handhold was just as likely to be a critical life-support instrument as a more innocuous point of erotic anchorage. One of these days, he was sure, he was going to make a dramatic grab for the Toilet Purge control in a thoughtless moment of climax.

Even in the ship's former life as a celebrity tour bus of extreme hyperluxury (before Myq had stolen both *it* and the small fortune required to convert it into a cargo-lugging haunt of egregious hyperweaponry – both, alas, from his former band mates) – even back *then* the service and control sections had been the claustrophobic haunt of cooks and crew; never a first-choice for venereal venues. Cockpit bonking, it was generally felt, was as tricky as it was tacky.

But with Teesa? With Teesa he'd never had to worry, and her present re-clinching manoeuvre was as impeccable as ever. Her perfect chest pivoted upwards with weightless momentum, her perfect jaw settling jigsaw-like against his shoulder.

On screen, holoheld above the liminals, the dustcloud from the wreck reached their shields and flared like a holy moment: a cheery radioactive death-rattle lent luminous form. The pair basked in the light, pausing for a moment in their exertions, weightless and sweating: he the supplicant, she the offering …

… then got bored of the pretentious bullshit and got back to biffing.

In many ways Teesa#32A[M/Tertius] was like a child. No getting around it – small in body and bearing. Yet somehow, Myq had noticed, able to contrive a general sense of *bigness*. She was nudging thirty, with black hair dyed artfully in toxic Mandelbrots of orange and pink and full-sleeve chromatophore tats set to cycle between three lurid patterns; her smile disarmed more effectively than any EM-spray; her eyes (whiskey and moss) flashed laser-hot at provocations serious or benign, and deep in their orbits lay some alien spark, some delightful hint of the remarkable.

She made Myq feel clumsy. Which he was. She made him – *me, the rock star! Her the backwater slave!* – feel provincial and naïve. Which he was. She made him feel big and slow and dull, which he was, which he was, which he was, and to *be* with her, to fuck her, to be dragged along in the sensory flotsam of her path… was to feel and experience and live in ways he'd never imagined.

So: there and then. Without thought, without precursor or anxiety, as detritus flamed and haloed, he said it.

'I love you. You hear me, Tee? I love you.'

He knew she'd smile at that, and she did. He knew she'd laugh, and she did. And then she kissed him twice, once on the tip of his nose and once on his bottom lip, both too quick for response, before getting back to arching, sighing, screaming.

Naturally, he laughed back. Not too loud, not too certain, slurping on the valve-tipped straw of a glamstimm as it spiralled by to cover the Awkward. *Too cool to care*, oh yes. He looped a gravless Happystrap™ round her thighs (top of the range, with a Riedquat mouse-fur lining and a four-page Satisfaction Guarantee – though nonetheless incapable of ever holding her still for long) and with its sturdy elasticity binding them got back to work.

Listen:

They'd screwed their way out of Alliance space like a snarling orgasmic bullet. From their first meeting in an ozone-reeking jail cell on Gateway, through all the aimless mosqui-toing of those first joyride weeks and the gradual turn towards

3

Federation territory, not a day had passed they didn't find some new way to rut, some novel mix of narcotics from the 'Geist's stores, some fresh merchant vessel to annihilate.

'Harder,' Tee whispered.

Today's unlucky victim was, *had* been, a chubby hauler. Glimpsed now past Tee's rolling shoulders it was difficult to make out any of the usual spotter's distinctions: size, berth, model, variant. Whatever denominative patterns might once have revealed its lineage were beautifully broken, straight lines sundered and angles abrogated, the unhappy crapheap recalling only the muddled traumas and splayed extremities of a huge flopping corpse.

'Harder. Harder, baby. Pleeease.'

Self-distract, Myq impulsed, detecting the first fuzzy warnings of a distant but building Early Ending. *The wreck. Self-distract. The wreck!*

Yeah, its shattered cavities yawning. A dead thing, a crippled giant: jagged modules disintegrating, all balletic momentum and weird parallax. Disparate threads of cable and duct eeling past in slow choreography like –

'Please …'

– *like innards*, he silently gurgled – poetically unhinged, obediently thrusting harder – *like the guts of a sacrifice smeared on a soothsayer's dish*.

Myq tended to get purple when stoned.

Even the ship's name was lost. It had stoically redacted its data-ID the instant the *Shattergeist*'s weapons went hot, and their first salvo had sublimated its nameplate: a chrysanthemum of gaseous metal momentarily visible amidst the blur, which had condensed in the void-chill just as fast. It jutted now, an eerie landscape, all fluted quills and misaligned stalactites. Like a detonation frozen in time, plated in silver.

4

Beautiful.

Predictably, the overworked Happystrap™ slid free. Teesa didn't notice. Myquel rearranged his grip and trajectory, diligently maintaining the pace, and tried again to mentally stave off the gathering eruption.

'Don't stop,' Tee huffed, unhelpful. 'Keep going. Ohhh, keep going.'

I'm bloody trying! he didn't say. *My old groupies were never this demanding.*

Instead he grunted something notionally affirmative and kept at it.

It was true though: he'd never had anyone like Teesa. Not, mind, that he'd had much opportunity to sample the more cosmopolitan breed of lover. The fanbrats who'd invariably mobbed him backstage at the height of his fame, those clumsily androgynous disciples of his shitty Microwave-Pop Folk revival, upon whom the entirety of his sexual education was based, were mostly just as green and lost as he'd been pretending he wasn't. His had been an audience of farm-fans and jut-toothed plantation prin-cesses, so enraptured by the band's arrival on whichever Interchangeable Rural Dungworld the tour had reached that they'd gamely tolerated his clueless dressingroom fum-blings then breathlessly thanked him. And *then*, *oh NoGod*, went stumbling with mascara running and lip-piercings a-wobble, gently informed that *no, sorry, we can't take you with us.* Back to their parochial offgrid little lives.

That, in the end, was the problem: the *smallness* of it all, the *realness* of it all. And hence precisely what had led Myq to that jail cell. And to her.

'There. Oh ffffuck. *There.*'

'But we need to get the scoop r—'

'Ssh. *There.*'

5

Still: it wasn't as if Teesa was some übersexed galactic sophisticate either. From what little Myq had gleaned of her past (mostly in that same copshop where they'd met), she hadn't left the Imperial moonlet where she'd been slaveborn until the day she stole her master's swankiest shuttle and blitzed for Alliance space. Whatever carnal brilliance she possessed was surely innate, instinctive: not the sort of thing (so Myq supposed) one learned from a life as an indentured chauffeur. It – '*it*' – poured out of her like viral music: something intangible, beyond attention; a subliminal code to light up the pleasure-centres and grid-nuke the balls. Demanding though she was, capricious and infuriating and contrary and mercurial though she was, Myq was never *not* horny while Teesa was around.

Distract. Distraaact!

Something, somewhere, chimed. A light blinked which hadn't before.

'What's—'

'Shut *up* shut *up* don't *stop*—'

He was close. Impossible to ignore now. Propelled sideways by Tee's throes he quickly lost sight of the unexpected light – and all the useful attention-diverting opportunities it had promised – so with a powerful instinct he instead clapped his eyes back onto the holo of the mangled hulk and tried to think unsexy thoughts.

The luckless ship had crossed their path just hours after their latest emergence from hyperspace. Myq had been worried about making another assault so soon after their last, and in a region so close. Only yesterday they'd gratuitously pulverised a fat Zorgon-line freighter, left it imploded and forlorn off the shoulder of Exphiay, and whatever authorities had bothered to respond to its squawking OhShit-beacons might conceivably still be close enough to catch wind of further violence.

But. Teesa had smiled. Teesa had said, 'AawwWWww,' and sulked. Teesa had jutted her lip and nibbled his neck and whispered, '*Pleeeeease, baby.*' And, dammit, as the hauler had shifted below them like an endless archiscape, as its unsuspecting pilots had hailed in a welter of voidjockey patois, Myq had mumbled:

'*Okay.*'

And Tee had unbuttoned his shirt. And they'd lit up their plasmaset while clothes ripped and tongues dug, and they'd picked their prey apart whooping and laughing and snorting and kissing and grinding and fucking and firing and firing and firing and firing and firing and firing and firing.

The chime rang out again. Just, alas, as Teesa decided to re-engage and re-position, showing herself off more fully, shooting Myq her most devastating smirk.

Think about something else, think about something else.

He subtly drifted them back towards the instruments. He wondered if the stricken crew of the hauler (he'd watched at least a few thrashing bodies tumble out, preserved in auto-deployed RemLok suits) had been stupid enough to spark their beacons while the *Shattergeist* lurked overhead. He was pretty sure – *pretty sure* – that he and Tee maintained an unspoken agreement that the object of their rampage was not so much randomly-perpetrated murder but the pointless and gratuitous destruction of big stupid spaceships (plus, sometimes, the shameless filching of any worthwhile cargo), but …

… but not quite sure enough, it was true, to risk drawing her attention to any post-eject drifters he noticed. Teesa never seemed to spot them herself (too busy admiring the wreckage, or fucking, or admiring the wreckage *while* fucking) and Myq instinctively avoided alerting her.

7

Gratuitous epic-scale destruction was one thing, strafing stragglers and salting the metaphorical earth felt like a step too far into the dark.

As if there's any going back now.

Still: a chiming chimey-thing was a chiming chimey-thing, a lit-up blinky thing was a lit-up blinky thing, and any responsible (*ha!*) captain (*ha!*) of any well-maintained (*ha!*) and properly licensed (*ha!*) craft owed it to him – or her – self to investigate. Even if he did happen to be off his tits on hormostimms. Or encumbered by the amorous attentions of a capricious sex fiend. Or even – no, *especially* – while actively attempting to delay ejaculation.

He squinted at the instruments, hunting the signal-light.

It was at this juncture that Teesa chose to throw back her head and howl like a wolf, which didn't help. Then to yelp and thrash and breathe, 'Yeah, yeah, yeah.' To clap ring-laden hands (she had a thing for trashy jewellery) onto his buttocks. And thereby to force him, as if she were operating some sort of fleshy rowing equipment, to up his tempo even further.

None of it, of course, conducive to anorgasmic sustainment.

Fortunately for Myq the blinking light more than came to his diversionary rescue. Less fortunately it did so by transmuting much of the approaching sexual volcanism into terror.

[LOC-PROX.] the holo-log began: an entry made thirty seconds earlier. **[FTL-EGRESSION.]**

Someone dumping themselves out of hyperspace in the stellar vicinity.

No biggie, Myq selfsoothed. *Could be anyone.*

[SCAN ALERT.] Twenty-five seconds ago.

It's fine. Everyone runs a local sweep after FTL. Common practice.

[NAV-POINT ASSOC: SHATTERGEIST HOMETAG.]

Seventeen seconds ago.

Someone … someone using us as a navigational fixed-point. That's … completely normal. Orientation procedure 101, no probl—

[INBOUND VECTOR.]

Ohhhh—

[SHATTERGEIST AUTOSCANNING INCOMING VESSEL.]

Don't be a cop please don't be a cop don't be a c—

[IDENT WITHHELD.]

Oh thank the almighty NoGod, cops have to self-ID, everyone knows th—

[ALERT: FIRING-SOLUTION DETECTED.]

No no no no—

[ALERT: MULTIPLE FIRING-SOLUTIONS DETECTED.]

'*Tee*, shit, Tee, stop, get off, we—'

Teesa hissed him to silence. Kept grinding and gripping with, impossibly, even greater urgency. His prick, against all neurophysical sense, unhelpfully failed to detumesce. Still he did his best to disentangle, to wriggle free, all while scrabbling blindly at ship controls he barely understood. And succeeding, evidently, only in exciting her even more.

'Teesa, seriously, someone's com—'

'Me.'

'Wh—'

'Me. I am. Me!'

'But—'

'Don't stop, don't you dare stop—'

'Ohfuck.'

On screen a glimmering blue dot drew a lazy contrail towards them, flickering with auto-detect infopings like camera-flash bursts, dragging to Myq's mind a memory of

9

that last show on Gateway. Glittering, sweaty, cheering swampworld Gateway where it all changed, where it all ended, where it all began. Gateway, where *Myq-L and the Bimblefunks* had played to their biggest crowd ever: a peristaltic ocean of pubescent shriekmonkeys clamouring through the Tumbledome, rending official vidshirts and rupturing their own throats. Gateway, which his promoters had relentlessly insisted was the Big One, the Biggest Of Them All, the hottest ticket out. Gateway, oh yes, where one could most efficiently access the communal hearts and wallets of its neighbouring cluster of loosely aggregated and only nebulously 'civilised' frontier worlds. And Gateway, which positively sloshed with the culture-starved barely-educated teenagers whose hormonal attention the rising star of Myq's celebrity had particularly captured.

But, oh, Gateway, where he'd nonetheless found himself overwhelmed, crushed, gloom-wrecked – by the sheer provincial crapness of it all.

'How are sales in Fed'-space?' he'd asked that night, sweat-drenched and underwear-pelted, as he stepped offstage. 'Did we chart?'

His managers had looked away.

The band didn't understand, of course – though each member had been dredged from a rustic morass similar to his own. Their perspectives had been overwhelmed within days of the tour's start. Each subsequent show (Bigger! Louder! More profitable!) had simply drawn them further into a punchdrunk paradise of infinitely exceeded expectations. To the others, Myq's frustrations, inarticulately ranted amongst the drug-packed leisure-suites the *Shattergeist* had once sported, had been bewildering at best and obscene at worst. Why couldn't he just be happy? Why couldn't he be satisfied with the adoration of his own stellar neighbourhood?

Why torture himself craving the consideration of the brand-frazzled, fad-guzzling, money-bleeding, numberless pop-sophisticates of the Federation? Why waste time and ambition on a doomed quest for the lasting respect of 300 billion infamously fickle trend-junkies halfway across the galaxy?

Myq had never really been able to answer that one. Mostly because it seemed so entirely bloody obvious it defied expression.

Because they're there.

That need to reach them all. That need to be known by them all. That need to transcend factionalism and achieve ... *what?*

Ubiquity. That was what. *No-tor-iety*.

... Yeah, *that* need, that need had poured piss onto any personal successes his brain deemed less than total.

There'd been a falling-out after the show. A touch of Dramatic Storming Out; a little too much of the famed local gin. A *lot* too much violent troublemaking around town and a seriously large amount of waking up in prison with a hangover like a Mephistophelian migraine.

Oh, it amounted to nothing in the end. Some overzealous policing by a crew of drugged-up, off-duty deputies, helped-along by Myq's sad habit of aggressive cuddling when drunk. It'd all settled quickly into a resolution pattern when he made his One Permitted Call and the cops realised he really was who he said.

('Frankly,' his prime-manager had buzzed down the line, 'it's exactly this sort of bad boy shit your brand needs.') He was duly instructed to sit tight and await the world-quaking starfall of his own personal apocalyptic megalaw-yers to arrange bail.

But in the interim?

11

In the interim he'd stared through the bars of the drunktank at the girl in the next cell ('*A slave abscondee,*' the cops muttered, suddenly acting weird, slurring even worse than when they'd found him, '*awaiting extradition to the Empire.*') all the while wondering why he'd developed a spontaneous erection.

… and all the while wondering how good a lawyer would have to be to spring out a band's, *say*, Personal Secretary, at the same time as its star.

'Hi,' he'd said through the bars, weirdly nervous. 'What's your name?'

Ha.

'Teesa number 32A!' squawked the voice which now filled the *Shattergeist*'s cockpit. 'M-for-Matteus, third intake-tranche, owner/patron Madrien Axcelsus!' An uninvited hail from the approaching vessel: to Myq's overburdened mind it struck like a raucous gong, forming words only by a quirk of acoustic probability. 'You are wanted for crimes too numerous to mention, principally … *ah* … corporate property-damage! Also homicide! You *will* sit tight or I *will* squash you!'

A man, Myq guessed, though it was difficult to be sure. All scrambled swagger and attitude.

'Bounty hunter,' Tee whispered. Still panting, still grinding, still slamming away as if everything were rosy. Still on the cusp of explosion. 'He'll kill us.'

Myq could hear the smile through her voice.

Insane. She's fucking insane.

'Rabbit?' he said.

'Rabbit,' she said.

They repositioned without debate. Still conjoined, still grinding; but at least now capable of reaching the liminals. Teesa wordlessly taking the pilot's set, both of them cradled against gees by the flight bench.

A warning shot ribboned past, accompanied by a gentle chirrup of alarm: a mag-accelerated projectile which grazed their shields before caroming into the wreck of the mangled freighter. A promise of more to come.

Teesa shuddered in his lap. An involuntary spasm of joy, he guessed, at the precise instant the missile hit metal. It segued neatly into a new fit of howling and whooping, and before Myq could respond or stabilise she'd reached out – quite deliberately – and struck a control on the dash.

[SHATTERGEIST: WEAPONS PRIMED.]

He probably would've protested – *no wait don't try to fight him he'll kill us he'll kill us he'll kill us* – if his power of speech hadn't been so profoundly robbed by exertion. So instead he thrust and steered and fired and laughed like a demon, and had just enough space, a calm lagoon beneath raging seas, to think:

I love her.

Sweet NoGod, I'm doomed.

On the console, like a beacon in fog, a second light had started to blink.

Two

Now, this one?

This one lived, if you can call it that, in the present. This one sat in the dark. This one watched an exchange of plasmic artillery bring gardens of light and colour to the void and tried, in the final cavity of her mind still capable of abstraction, to remember the last time she'd smiled.

Difficult to know. Harder to care.

SixJen. Her name (she still had one) was SixJen. Tall and brown and bald as a beetle, she sat straight and toyed unthinking with a pistol flechette: the toothed, hollow-tipped breed she favoured when forced to fight *out there*.

In the Real. As in: among *people*.

Her ship – the *The* – flopped imperfectly over itself and yawed lazily to port: a supremely choreographed part of its starring turn as Piece Of Debris #236. Other, more legitimate members of its company, lumps and cords of unrecognisable slag, metallic viscera from the murdered freighter, shunted and dispersed on either side, masking her drift. Nonetheless, as a precautionary measure, the *The*'s systems had been dialled as low as possible: preserving all detectable traces of heat.

SixJen the killer played possum and stared at her half-sleeping sensors.

On screen the oblivious combatants coiled and danced amidst ghostly vectors of radiation, as if performing for her sole delight. As if she was still capable of being delighted.

'Got style-profiles for you,' a voice said. Its tinny inflection (suggestive, SixJen always thought, of scurrying rodents), somehow contrived to sound both insolent and bored. 'Partial, anyway. If you're interested.' It insinuated itself about the dreary cockpit without obvious source.

She almost frowned.

'Define "partial", Lex.' *Her* voice, naturally, was an unaffected monotone.

'Well, okay ... the merc? He's nothing special. Look – am I right? 'Course I am.' If it had possessed a body the speaker might well have preened, at that. 'He's better than most flyers, maybe, fine, sure ... But ...'

... but SixJen could already see what the little voice was driving at. The bounty hunter who'd so flashily interrupted her exquisite stalking of the *Shattergeist* was a deft combatant, no doubt. She could smell the competence in every hard turn of his ship (*a classic-spec Cobra III*, she noted, *heavy on speed and explodo-mods; light on shields and daintier deadlies*) and in every swanky chaff-dodging barrel-roll he made. He knew when to thumb back and when to max-gee, could anticipate and pre-empt the fugitive ship's attempts to bolt, and could cling grimly to its tail when it weaselled and wove into the debris-field still inflating around them.

And yet, and yet ... like the specs of his kit, like the theatre of his entrance, even like the paintjob he'd inflicted on his bird – all gloss-black and gold chevrons – SixJen could detect in his every line, every move, every switch and salvo, a singular lack of imagination.

'... but nothing special.' She finished Lex's line for him.

It always irked her, in some distant way, to agree with the little voice. A sensation *it* didn't help by audibly sniggering.

SixJen's nearlyfrown turned actual. Smugness, she held, was not an appropriate affectation for a machine. She

15

groped for the tiny disc on her lapel which constituted Lex's brain – 90% microsensors, 10% infuriatingly-programmed whiny ersatz-personality core, all currently diverted via the ship's sleepy systems – and repeated her command while flicking its shell.

'Define … *"partial"*.'

'All right. *Ow*! Fuck's sake! All right!' The little computer often reacted, she'd noticed, as if capable of feeling pain. Just another idiotic impersonation of life – like everything it said – but a useful means, nonetheless, of bringing it back on topic. 'I meant the rabbit, right? The runner. It keeps … shifting pattern. Can't get a proper profile. No predictable strategy, no emergent trend. Schizophrenic flying.'

Right again.

On screen, in and around a zone of heavy debris – close to where the *The* hung inert – the *Shattergeist* flowed and flipped like a bright bead on a squall: as graceful as it was chaotic. In spite of its polished aesthetic the gold-class yacht (SixJen could recognise the curves and phallic body of an SK 'Dolphin' pleasureboat, even beneath the crazed welter of fins and lobstered plates someone insane, tasteless and wealthy had used to accessorise it) was built for comfort, not combat. And yet the *Shattergeist* described a course of inconsistent loops and lunges which decried its prolate build. In one phase it corkscrewed among the stellar junk like a dragonfly: soft course-tweaks suggesting a pilot of such instinctive prescience SixJen didn't spot a single crumb of contact-flare on its bow, nor any but the most unnecessarily awesome deployments of the bounty hunter's arsenal depleting its shield. And then, just as effectively, without warning, it assumed the role of a stellar thug: shouldering aside detritus to scatter walls of white-hot rubble into its pursuer's path.

'She's good,' SixJen intoned.

Only Lex – after long years of experience in what passed for SixJen's body-language – might have detected the shadow of a whiff of a ghost of admiration in her voice. Perhaps even a frisson of concern. Fortunately, via lessons learned long ago, he wasn't in the habit of mentioning it.

'You're sure it's her at the wheel?' he chirruped. 'Not the patsy? This … this rock star guy?'

'It's her.'

'So what action?'

A twinned bubble of lightflares whited-out the holo's gain. The first was one of two grossly overloaded Killkure™ plasma bombs the *The*'s scanners had spotted aboard the merc's Cobra, sublimating several tonnes of vac-borne spacetrash. The second, somewhat less elegant, was the Cobra itself: shunting brutally into a cunningly-deposited lump of dazzlechaff the fugitive had dumped during combat. By the time the screen had compensated for both glarespots the two ships had emerged with shields bleeding antineutrinos and hulls trendily distressed, but otherwise unharmed. And resumed their maddening dance.

'No action,' SixJen said. 'We wait.'

This, after all, was the game. The game as she chose to play it.

No excitement. No rush.

Let the other competitors show themselves. Let them be exhausted and drained by the chase. Let them chip away at the prey until both are panting and weakened. Let them lower their guards. Let them stand, swords steaming, beside the lake beneath the tree with the golden bough—

And then.

Then!

Lex made a point of clearing the throat he didn't have. 'There is, *ah* … one thing …'

17

'Mm?'

'You're doing it again.'

SixJen glanced down, knowing instantly what he meant. Sure enough, a ragged red line welled from a cut along the back of her forearm: one edge of the flechette's sharpened fins pricking in for a second pass. A tube of blood, untroubled by gravity, sat over the wound like a crimson worm, rippling longitudinally, waiting for its own surface tension to fail. She glared at it, at what she'd done to herself, with a faint flicker of shame: a sensation so unfamiliar that it perversely engendered an equal and opposite buzz of savage pride –

I can still feel!

– both of which Actual Emotions so overwhelmed her that she swiped away the blood without thinking, scattering a small swarm of glinting, weightless rubies to shatter and circulate through the cockpit.

Her annoyance at *that*, depressingly, barely registered.

Numb. In and out. And worse every day.

She clamped a hand to the wound, covering it and the countless others – some scabbed, some scarred – already whorling across the back of her right arm, noting that even on self-destructive autopilot her brain had been coldly rational enough not to slice too deep. In silent comparison she stole a glance at the back of her *other* arm. *The holy one.* No crazy crisscross there. No messy displacement guiltily recorded on tea-tone skin.

The left arm, no, was not a canvas for the Casual Doodle.

But still: it had its display of scars. Seven, in all. Deeper, more deliberate; each a puckered pair of thin keloid lips. Five she'd collected in person. The second victim, and the fourth, had each already accounted for one other apiece, hence seven. She'd gained most of them from back near

18

the start, back when the chase seemed fresh and fierce, before the empty spaces and the creeping cold.

Seven down. Four still out there.

It had never lasted this long before.

She returned her gaze to the holo and shuttered down her eyes. The dogfight, she noted, was growing even dimmer.

'We're drifting out of range,' Lex supplied. 'You want me to get us cl—'

'I'll do it.'

She flew perfectly, of course. A few exquisite tweaks, a few directional nudges to affect a course-change, parroting a Brownian-buffeting by other nearby junk, to carry them softly back towards the battle. So deft was her touch that the *The* barely lifted from its sleeper-state: expenditures of heat so faint that none but the most grotesquely refined systems could have detected them, and even then only by pilots undistracted by the more pressing concerns of mortal combat.

More sharply defined now by proximity, the merc's Cobra was maintaining a constant stream of kinetic destruction: every fifth shell a blazing tracer, every twentieth a rad-dirty klikbug to help his vectoring. SixJen watched him tailspin from an outfacing loop to intercept the runner as it came back round – and for one hateful second she was certain he'd done it: had outflown the fugitive, had smuggled a direct line onto its least shielded front-facing aspect. But the clever little move paid no dividends. Even as the Cobra poured fire and tweaked for its strike the *Shattergeist* had already shifted out of alignment: a crash-halt followed by a monodirectional burst from a dorsal thruster. It simply dropped perpendicular to the combat, like an anchor into an abyss – precisely the sort of spatial sneakiness which marked out the born spacejockey from the glorified atmoflyer.

19

'Huh,' Lex declared. Algorithmically impressed.

Far worse for the hunter, as he flopped and struggled to regain his line, was a massive slab of the dead freighter which came bumbling from the mass to fragment across his starboard fluke.

Shitty luck, SixJen thought without sympathy. Quietly self-censoring the arising notion that the *Shattergeist*'s eccentric moves might have been leading to this all along. *Nobody's that good.*

The shields on the merc's Cobra held up, though barely, and the monstrous wreckage crumbled around them like an icesheet striking flame. But in all the foaming ionic chaos the Cobra's inertia was annihilated, and it tumbled back from the collision with the selfsame force it was so flam-boyantly expending to survive.

And then the turn.

In that one moment of shieldlight and confusion, as the hunter grappled with unhelpful physics and hurried to recharge his shield, the *Shattergeist* had all the time in the world to bolt. To max-gee out of range and start pounding out the warpjumps: testing the chaser's ability to follow, widening the lag in a great, glorious chase across inconceiv-able space. SixJen herself sat poised to pursue.

But the *Shattergeist* didn't move.

Lex parroted a pointless intake of nonbreath. 'Are they …?'

It opened fire.

Seeping open hotmodded bays which the *The*'s scanners hadn't even spotted, the so-called pleasure yacht coughed out a bright volley at its tormentor.

'Closer,' SixJen whispered, feeling something – something so tiny it was barely there – akin to surprise. She was happy to let Lex handle the tweaks this time, more concerned

with the show. Determined to be ready, but ... yes.
Off-balance.

The runner was *not* supposed to scheme.

The runner was *not* supposed to plan.

Still, for all the cocksure precociousness of the *Shattergeist*'s assault, it was about as stupid a move as its pilots could have taken. Flashy, spectacular, heroic – suicidal.

Element of surprise. Unpredictable behaviour. All well and good, but never quite as effective as a top-spec suite of hyper-destructive nuclear overkill and a ship (a top-spec Cobra Mk. III, say, in gloss black and gold) built like a toxic arrowhead. Hence the merc barely noticing the *Shattergeist*'s whiny little salvo.

Bit by bit the Cobra stopped spinning. Regained its poise. And yawed like a tilted compass towards its prey.

SixJen felt something shift along her neck. The fine hairs there, reacting dumbly to an adrenal quickening her mind had long since forgotten how to feel. Whoever he was, however pissy or humiliated or (for all she knew) aroused he might be by the long predictable fight and the short unpredicted lesson in Being Made To Look Like A Rookie, the bounty hunter did the one and only sensible thing he could.

He fired everything.

Missiles flew, scratching chalky contrails to fizz and disperse in instants. Cannon flared their weird airless puffs of muzzlelight and lead. A pair of clunky railguns heaved uranium splinters so fast the *The*'s systems couldn't track them, stabbing so acutely at the *Shattergeist*'s shield that SixJen could see it buck backwards with her naked eye.

... and because the lunatics in the fugitive craft had so obligingly turned their nose towards the hunter to enable their spasm of return fire, this whole ghastly bombardment, this whole grim curtain of heat and atomic decay, thundered upon the bow of the *Shattergeist* like a cosmic shroud, wrapping and choking its body, erasing its shields in jigsaws of energetic collapse. The fields choked and died long before the barrage was spent, leaving its final stages to gouge directly at the yacht's armour.

'Multiple direct hits,' Lex pointlessly announced, bulbous lights tearing and deforming across the scanner. 'Their shields're fucked. Main engine's gone cold. They're driftwood.'

Still the self-consuming fireballs. Still the rail-shot ripping at ablative sheets. The *Shattergeist* dervished and puked chaff with every strike, and SixJen made a conscious effort not to grind her teeth. Not to reach for the controls.

Don't kill them, she willed. *Don't you kill them, you shit. Not yet.*

They're mine.

In all of this SixJen the killer was trusting, and worse still risking *everything* in that trust, that her impressions of the nameless merc were accurate; that in all his swagger and bombast he wouldn't simply vaporise his targets. That he'd be content with first crippling them … with stealing closer to gloat. And that, if he had even the slightest sense, he'd already spotted the value of the *Shattergeist* and its upgrades and was at this moment, like any smart businessman, smelling the money …

She couldn't take them both. Not at the same time. But one weakened enemy after another?

That was the game. *Those* were the odds.

The storm faded at last. A few diaphanous webs of chemical fire lingered for an instant, drawing back from the battered yacht like wings, then died away. SixJen didn't bother asking Lex about life signs. If she'd miscalculated, if the fugitive was dead, she would have known it already.

22

'We got range?' she whispered, unable to stop herself glancing down at her left arm. The seven scars.

'Surely do. At current drift ... let's see ... closest pass is in three minutes. Out of range four after that.' Lex, as ever, sounded inappropriately chipper. 'You want me to start sl—'

'Just stand by. I say the word and we go hot. All the way hot.'

'Yep. We got some more comm-traffic out there, by the way.'

'Let's hear it.'

A shrill sound expanded into the cockpit, so abrupt and abrasive SixJen autotwitched for her pistol.

Screaming.

Something akin to panic, muffled deep down, swarmed into her. *The rumer's hurt! She's dying! How does it work if she just bleeds to d—*

She stopped herself. Listened a little closer to the voice.

Yes: unmistakably female, and yes: unmistakably shrieking. But ...

(Lex sniggered out loud.)

But not in pain.

SixJen cleared her throat. 'They're ... they're broadcasting this at the Cobra?'

'Uh-huh. They got no idea we're intercepting. Heh ... Excitable little thing, isn't she? Oh, wait, here we go, matey's just opened a line too ...'

Another voice. The same scrambled pomp-merchant mercenary who'd announced his arrival with such fanfare before.

'Occupants of ... occupants of the *Shattergeist* ...' it said, all but drowned by the shrieks. Even SixJen, generally blind to behavioural nuance, could hear the man's awkwardness.

23

'A-as a licensed agent of the Pilots' Federation I'm … I'm here to claim a bounty placed on … on …'

The orgasmic cries modulated down into something more akin to the mewing of a hysterical cat. SixJen thought she could make out a deeper voice behind it, grunting along in time.

'Look,' said the bounty hunter. 'Look, if you could … if you'd just stop that for a second and listen, I'd …'

'*Oh ffffuuuuuuuuuuuuuuckhereitcomesagaaaaainnn—*'

'I'm … I'm trying to throw you a lifeline, you little shits! The PF's got six grand on you – cuffed or carrion. I'm just … I'm just thinking maybe you send me on my way with … with a …'

SixJen permitted herself a single, professional nod. *Smelling money.*

But the fugitives either weren't listening or didn't care.

'Last chance!' the merc hissed, frustration bubbling through the scrambler. 'I have a three-ton plasmic warhead *right here,* and unless y—'

SixJen killed the signal with a flicker. *Heard enough.*

Took a deep breath.

'Lex?'

'Present.'

Another breath. *Hold it. Try to feel it.*

(*Try to feel* anything.)

Pointless.

'Go hot.'

The *The* awoke around her. Stabilisers shields sensors guns guns *guns* every every *everything* all at once, whirring and rushing to life. A vituperative ghost casting off its sheets. A baleful red heat-return winking open on her enemies' screens.

'Kill him.'

The rush. The fuming ragesounds of munitions ripping from pods, tubes venting lancets of compact hell. (There was a time she'd found this part thrilling.)

Now she just sniffed and fiddled with the flechette.

In the end the Bounty Hunter lasted less than a minute. In all the startled confusion of a newly emerged threat (she imagined him swearing and stumbling, alarms croaking, lights blaring, struggling to reorient and respond) he barely got off a single shot. His cannon were still incandescent from the dogfight, his railguns left stupidly unloaded, his shields still coughing from the debris collision. He'd thought himself alone. Alone with a defenceless victim, a single fucknormous Killkure™ missile and no need to consider anything else.

The *The* had flickered to life behind his back like a piece of scenery, some dreary inanimate *nothing* safely disregarded, and spat fiery poison through his spine.

Unfair.

(She might have coughed out a bitter laugh at that, once.)

A plasma volley to finish cooking his shields: precisely the sort of shock-and-awe bullshit he understood. And then the real business. A fusillade of tungsten-tipped javelins accelerated to near-C inside the *The*'s portly chest: relativistic doombullets that slipped through the Cobra's skin like needles and erased (not exploded, not shredded, simply *removed*) whatever vital organs they punctured: dragging along all sublimated remnants in their irresistible wake. Weapons pods, chaff-bays, engines, life-support, tac-systems. The Cobra was disarmed, hamstrung, disembowelled and dissected.

Carved.

Spacedeath, the methodical way.

Still: *credit where due.* The bounty hunter had had the presence of mind to bail, at least. He hung now, an

25

aggravated little maggot, flexing impotently in his RemLok beside the crippled cadaver of his ship. SixJen ignored the pinging of his OhShit-beacons and turned the great pregnant knuckle that was the *The* towards its real prey.

(Ohhhh, the *The:* the closest she'd ever come to a treasure; an object of pride; a lover. *Lakon Asp, Mk. II.* Unpainted. Unbeautiful. No sleek edges, no aquiline affectations, no go-faster stripes or stupid fucking fins. A wide-shouldered bitch with a fabulously unimaginative name which was so elaborately packed with hidden killtech it was worth, at last count, roughly eight times the basic model it was pretending to be. A devil dressed as a tramp.)

'Weapons're recharged,' Lex said, anticipating her command. 'You want me to hail 'em first?'

Another tingle on her neck. She felt …

… *well*: she felt nothing. Naturally. And yet surreally was aware that at this point she should be breathless, should be quivering at the imminence of a decade-overdue climax. The dissonance was dizzying.

'Open a line.'

This time the audio ruckus from the *Shattergeist* had shifted from screams to laughter: two voices so thoroughly intertwined in sleepy happiness and post-coital self-congratulation it was hard to know where one ended and the other began.

'Hey,' SixJen made out from the fug, 'hey, there's … *ha.* There's spunk all in the life-support.'

'Occupants of the *Shattergeist*,' she said. 'I salute you. Please prepare to die.'

More laughter.

SixJen sighed. Leaned slightly. Brought her mouth closer to the tiny bud of the *The*'s comms-mic. And said the word.

No more than a sound, really. Not meant for regular ears. A thing of weird resonance and disturbing echoes.

The laughter from the *Shattergeist* stopped. SixJen allowed herself a glimmer of satisfaction at that. *She knows.*

'Tee?' came the man's voice. 'Tee, you okay? You look wei—'

'It's fine.' *Her. The runner. The runner's voice.*

SixJen closed her eyes. Braced herself. *At last.*

At last!

She wished, distantly, she could've felt some satisfaction in the moment. But then, it didn't matter much. In just a moment it wouldn't matter at all.

She opened her eyes and began to reach for the weapons.

From the *Shattergeist* the voice said, 'Let me just ... Here. Move your leg, ok? That's it. Hold on a sec.'

Something *pinged*.

'Um,' Lex squawked. 'Shit.'

Afterwards, when the *Shattergeist* was gone, when Lex had finished swearing and SixJen had stopped telling him to stop, numbly aware he was simply approximating the emotions she couldn't feel herself, the full picture achieved dreadful solidity.

A mist of debris rattled around their ship.

'They have a mag-gun,' Lex growled.

'Yes.'

'And scan-breakers.'

'Yes.'

'They never lost their fucking shield, did they?'

'No.'

'Or their engine.'

'No.'

'They pretended.'

'They did.'

'You ... you think they clocked us drifting in from the start?'

'I think they clocked us from the start.'

Lex hmm'ed. Then:

'They shot that prick's Killkure™, didn't they?'

'They shot that prick's Killkure™.'

The *Shattergeist* had syruped off into a warpspace gravitywell even as the merc's dead Cobra, hanging beside the *The*, was rendered to atoms by the primed payload still lodged inside it. Sniped perfectly by a sexcrazed maniac.

(A dying audio-signal from the fugitive, as it dopplered away to white noise, had faithfully broadcast the male passenger's whimper at the woman's cheerful observation that, *oh look*, he was Getting Stiff Again.)

Thus ignominiously evaded, SixJen hadn't wasted time fretting over her own safety. The fearsome wash of molecular waste and collateral debris was effortlessly deflected by the *The*, lighting up shields in great opaque sprays. But for every moment it sat braced against the tsunami, senseblind and tide-tossed, the spout of exotic particles left by the *Shattergeist* dispersed, taking with them SixJen's only shot at tracking it into hyperspace. By the time the slightest useful visibility was restored the signature was a dying wisp, and even then the stellar ash from the Cobra's cremation, alive with obfuscatory EM-returns and corruptive radiation, would confound any attempt to pursue the prey for long minutes to come.

No … SixJen didn't need Lex's talent for stating the obvious to grasp the simple truth.

The *Shattergeist* was gone.

'She's good,' the killer whispered, thoughtlessly slicing at her right arm.

By way of afterthought:

The other merc was barely alive. Cooked in his cockpit,

then irradiated in his RemLok. SixJen was obliged to suit-up just to interrogate him in the vac-clean mouth of the *The*'s cargo scoop.

Unmemorable face. A name she'd never heard. A Pilots' Federation account unworthy of distinction.

She said the word to him, just in case. He stared blankly, uncomprehending, through his visor.

So she shot him through the face, shoved him back into space, and returned to the darkness inside.

No fresh scar on her left arm today.

Three

Now?

Now Myq held Teesa's hand and stared into a dozen apathetic faces, plus at least as many SenseNet lenses, in an undecorated conference room aboard the Federation Coriolis station affectionately known as 'Tun's Wart' – LaGrange-locked between the unremarkable Tun/Ton binaries near Exbeur. He smirked with a confidence he didn't feel.

'We,' he declared, adopting the same insouciant drawl he'd used to loosen wallets and knickers back home, 'are destructertainment.'

The journalists failed to look impressed.

Balls, Myq thought.

The lovers had detected the first incipient stirrings of mass attention, of notoriety, of – *say it* – celebrity, a couple of weeks after the Incident with the bounty hunters. Since the adrenal buzz of that combat they'd spent every non-erotic moment arguing over the merits of their preferred strategies, schizophrenically managing to pursue both, back and forth, according to whoever's was the prevailing voice at any given moment. In phases when Teesa was the more persuasive (generally when assisted by narcotics and naked-ness) a traditional pattern was observed: locate cargo vessel, smash to itty bits, buy more ammo and upgrades, repeat *ad infinitum*. Whenever Myq's preferred policy was in the ascendancy (generally when Tee was asleep or their crotchal regions were too distressed to bear another assault) the *Shattergeist* pursued a more conservative manifesto: running a long way from the scene of their most recent outrage, refuelling, then running some more.

The battle had shaken Myq in ways Tee would've mocked if he'd admitted them. The smug merc, the ruined Cobra, and then that second hunter (*for NoGod's sake!*) popping up like a sheep-guzzling alpharhyncus disguised as a fucking boulder.

Blowing Shit Up, Myq had concluded, was undeniably thrilling, and Not Being Blown Up Oneself was undeniably the preferred partner strategy. But *Almost* Being Blown Up …? Coming Within A Gnat's Bollock Of Being Blown Up? He hadn't decided yet how he felt about that, and had defaulted in the interim to a strategy of unthinking avoidance.

Tee, typically, who'd been at the controls throughout the whole fight, in spite of a theatrically protracted orgasm, had thought the whole thing glorious fun.

But now? Now Myq would've jumped at the chance to be locked in a hellatious dogfight, missiles inbound and shields failing, if it meant he could just escape the sweaty silence of this so-called press conference.

'"*Destructertainment*",' one of the journalists echoed, as if sampling the word. A clammy little man at the rear with a backgammon hat and a camlens implanted above his left eye, he packed into that one repetition a sophisticated combination of complex and well-considered derision and disgust. Along the way it absorbed into its specific articles of mockery a more general package of revulsion aimed, so Myq neurotically intuited, at the lovers' undeserved self-importance, their grimy clothing, his own backwater accent, and all the associated rural triviality his very being implied.

31

Myq was feeling unusually sensitive today, and dimly suspected he knew why.

He'd never had to share Tee's attention with anyone before.

'Um,' he said. 'Yeah. Destructertainment. That's right.'

The little man whistled a mad melody under his breath and heavy-lidded his eyes. 'Destructertainment,' he repeated. Then whistled again.

Tee gripped Myq's hand harder. The word, like this whole thing, had been her idea. Ironically enough it had been during one of the 'avoiding-all-trouble' stretches, drifting out in the spatial boondocks, while Tee lazed like a cat and he rubbed anti-chafe meds onto his nethers, that they'd got their first inkling of the media fallout from their spree. Cycling through lowband newsies and one or two highband bulletins from the local cluster, he caught reference to their destructive excesses three times within an hour. In each case the *Shattergeist*'s shenanigans were reported with all the requisite outrage he'd expect of the morally-vanilla newsnets – '*wanton and obscene destruction!*' '*no obvious motive!*' '*not a single thought spared for collateral damage!*' – and yet in each case there was also a *hmm*-provoking note of incongruity.

In the first clip, for instance, after all the fire-and-brimstone stuff, the story segued into an indignant medley of vox pop soundbytes, amidst whose predictable condemnations and sighs ('*What's the galaxy coming to?*') a couple of younger voices announced they thought the footage of the *Shattergeist* looked 'actually kinda supernebular', and bluntly proposed there were worse things one could do with one's time than shit on the profit-margins of the megacorps.

'Huh,' Myq had said, squirting more ointment.

The second broadcast was a glitzier, vid-complete affair whose visual element switched between a glossy anchorwoman and various blackbox recordings (from the victims' POV, naturally) of the *Shattergeist* in action. It upped the ante by not only naming the fugitive vessel directly, but the Alliance-space 'pop-band' from whom it'd been reported stolen. And then, the pertinent signal amidst the noise, it signed-off with a weird Public Safety message imploring parents to prevent their kids from stealing ships in an attempt to emulate the criminals.

Which, Myq pondered, *sort of implies some of them already tried* …

The third piece, audio only, was so drearily condemnatory he almost switched it off prematurely. But as the report ended and clangy adolescent MehRap artfully faded-up to replace it, the newscaster, unaware his mic was still live, blurted, 'Ya know what? That sounds like a lotta fun. Those kids're okay by m—'

The feed died as swiftly as an anonymous producer could flip a switch.

'People,' Myq had murmured to himself, articulating a piece of bloody obvious wisdom as if in receipt of a holy epiphany, 'really like seeing shit getting blown up.'

Tee had merely farted softly from the bunk in the corner, chromatophore tattoos flashing yellow and purple, and giggled in her halfsleep. But when she woke …?

When she awoke: *the idea.*

This … bloody … idea.

Outstaring a roomful of confused contemptuous journalists and trying to monetise madness.

'Is this,' said the sweaty little reporter, he of the crap hat and the sophisticated interpersonal expression of contempt, 'a joke?'

'Save your questions for the end, please,' Tee inserted. They'd agreed Myq was going to do the talking (for reasons he could neither remember nor currently fathom) but as Tee stepped forwards with hands on hips he could see the effect she carried with her – '*it*', the *thing*, the *change* – stealing over the assembled hacks like a toxin. One by one they forgot him, their arched brows softened away, their apathy was drowned in enchantment. Some licked their lips. One woman fiddled thoughtlessly with her hair. At least one man, Myq was sure, absent-mindedly adjusted his own undercarriage.

Tee smiled sweetly. She was good at that.

'I know you're wondering why you're here,' she said. 'I know you must have low expectations. Yesterday we extended an invitation to every journal, castnet and two-bit tabloid in this system. A press conference hosted by persons unknown, regarding matters undisclosed. Not very promising, is it? *Ha*. No. But, oh! Oh, you came.'

She chose not to state aloud the implied reality: that anyone dispatched by a hateful editor on just such a fool's errand must surely be the lowliest, most internally despised wordmonkey on any given payroll. The assembly, Myq liked to think, were grateful for that kindness.

'You came,' she trilled. 'You came, and I want to thank you. From the bottom of my heart –' she brushed a hand across her own chest – 'thank you for coming.'

Myq caught himself watching her with the same fascination, the same weird semi-aroused hang-on-every-word reverence, as the journos. It was the precise brain-obfuscation he'd become so willingly accustomed to, nothing new there, but he'd never truly seen her like this. Never heard her sharing words with more than one listener. Never known her to stay on one topic for more than a few mercurial seconds, let alone lasso a crowd with such empty charm and clumsy innuendo.

'Thank you for coming,' she whisper-repeated, innocently wetting her lips.

(One of the journos, a woman, actually moaned.)

She's hypnotised us, he thought. And then felt bizarrely, horribly, unforgivably, jealous at having to share it.

'So,' Tee finished with the reasoned air of someone who'd had the last word in a disagreement but didn't want to gloat. 'We'd like to reward you for taking that chance.'

She nodded at Myq—

Me! Nobody else! Fuck you guys!

—and he tapped a control set into the lectern. Tee gestured expansively at the projectorama behind them, leading eyes and cameras in an obedient swivel.

Above, in glorious oblate holodepth, footage from the *Shattergeist*'s senselogs zoetroped through an endless loop of explosions, strafes, mag-snipes and manufactured collisions. Three weeks and fifteen ships: freighters, cargo runners, two shuttles, an obese managerial pleasure liner (empty, it later transpired) and a colossal steely wreck half-salvaged by a corporate grinder-crew which the pair had blown up just for the hell of it. Into the mix they'd edited more intimate shots from the interior of the *'Geist*'s cockpit: the lovers laughing, cheering, kissing; reacting with passion and poignancy to the parade of artisanal destruction.

But nothing sordid, Myq thought, stifling a sarcastic smirk. *NoGod forbid we should offend anyone.*

This, the pair had agreed, splicing footage of catastrophe and carnage, should be a montage fit for a family show.

'Destructertainment,' Myq heard himself say again, weirdly loyal to Tee's ugly term.

'Destructertainment,' she repeated, her hand again finding his.

And, yeah, this time:

35

'… destructertainment,' the reporters mumbled. Nodding along. Loosening collars, wiping brows. Partly, Myq supposed, they were in shock: they'd had the unexpected good fortune of the region's newest novelty presenting itself to them on a platter. But mostly?

Mostly, it's her.

Smiling. Watching them like an artist unveiling her opus. And just as she basked in their wonder, so they basked in her.

Most of them.

The sticky guy at the back, Myq had observed, had barely glanced at the destruction on screen. Something about him, surpassing even his condescending little turn before, prickled at the base of Myq's spine.

'You will have noticed,' Tee was saying, with the same calm tone one might use to address a company of wayward teenagers, 'that you can't livecast from this room. That's nothing to worry about.' Several of the journos had indeed dreamily reached to fiddle with cameras and mictech, their adoration briefly polluted by a note of consternation. 'Lead in the walls. And some sort of scrambler signal, I don't really understand it myself. But, please, we're more than happy for you to record everything you see. You'll appreciate we'd simply like to be well on our way before any transmissions actually occur.'

Despite the sizeable dent this restriction put in the journos' pursuit of a scoop, still they nodded and smiled with foggy understanding. *Good, horny, sluggish little puppets.*

Every Coriolis station in Federation space, so it transpired, had a room like this. After decades of frostwar with the Empire, replete with intelligence scares, political scandals and unhelpful tech-innovation, it had been belatedly agreed by those in command that the easiest way to obviate paranoia was simply to ensure VIPs were never far from a wall without ears. Despite the prohibitive costs of installing such data-sanctuaries station owners had rushed to cough-up for a 'Whispering Room' of their own, sensing with mercantile glee the opportunity to charge equally extortionate amounts for rental and use. There was never a shortage of people with secrets.

The hacks accepted the news of their non-immediacy without grumble. In fact the longer they spent in the room the more their professional decorum, the bulldog loyalty to their particular rag, the unspoken enmity and competition which had crackled between them at first, eroded in the tidal wash of Tee's performance. On one side a man was now openly fondling the buttocks of the gentleman in front, while a couple in the centre, professional nemeses for all Myq knew, kept leaning together to exchange lusty kisses before remembering themselves and breaking apart. Then forgetting again.

Watching, Myq caught himself stifling a grin more than once, until the dread suspicion occurred that he was simply regarding his own fate from the outside: that these people were no different from him; that he, like them, was enslaved, ensorcelled, enchained, by the mad urge to dance to Teesa's tune.

And hot on the heels of that revelation: the inevitable *How?*

And just as inevitably, like all questions of pertinence which arose in Teesa's presence, the query was annihilated before it could germinate. This time, at least, not by Tee herself.

The sweaty man in the hat bolted for the exit.

Wants his fucking scoop!

Myq shifted on instinct to chase, realising instantly it was hopeless. And grasping, somewhat slower, the full weight of the disaster that would arise from as small a thing as a man opening the door. The data-sanctuary would collapse. The battery of cams and transmitters would, with automatic obedience, start livecasting all they'd seen.

And then: cops.

And then: shooting.

And then: the end.

(Myq wasn't sure, abstractly, if 'the end' he was concerned about was 'of life' or 'of the adventure', but it didn't seem quite the right time for comparative analysis. Somehow it never did, when Teesa was around.)

The hat man reached the threshold. Cast a manic hand towards the slidelock.

And slammed to a halt with an undignified squeak.

On the wall beside him, three federal inches from the side of his face, a perfect dandelion of soot and metal cooled with a glassy crackle and a puff of smoke. The man stared at it, trembling. And then twisted, along with Myq and every autolens in the room, towards Teesa.

Where did she get a fucking gun ...?

She slipped it back into a pocket, a half-glimpsed laser gadget in pink and vomit-green, and smiled innocently.

'Let's try to keep toilet breaks until the end, shall we? We have a lot to get through.'

The man shuffled back to the pack, avoiding every eye. Once again whistling his sad little tune.

'We're here today,' Tee said, ignoring him, 'to tell your viewers, listeners and readers about an exciting money-spending opportunity. Myq?'

Heads turned towards him. He gaped once or twice, still floundering in the electric atmosphere of A World Where Tee Has A Fucking Gun, and then surrendered to the spell. Went with the flow.

Same old, same old.

'It's remarkably simple,' he said. 'On screen behind me now you'll notice a code number. That's an account held at the First Bank of Intangia: a clever little concern nominally registered on the Independent world Bohmshohm but in fact lacking for branches, headquarters or … well, any premises at all. Which is to say: not somewhere the Federation can go and get antsy.

'So what we'd really like is for you, you at home, hi, nice to meet you, for you to send a bunch of money to that account. Which we'll then basically use to carry on doing what we're doing now. That is: blowing up ships belonging to the unbelievably wealthy corporate arsebags whose influence affects every last part of your lives.' He smiled. ''Cos it's expensive, that sort of thing.'

Renting signal-proof conference rooms, for instance.

Not having the criminal connections required to sell stolen stock wherever we go, for instance.

Constantly multiplying, upgrading and reloading the ferocious armaments of a once-luxurious tour ship, for instance.

Buying blackmarket pink-and-green laserguns without fucking telling me, for fucking instance.

'In exchange for this act of generosity, we'll make sure we send all the tasty footage from said acts of Blowing Corporate Stuff Up onwards to the very same journalists from whom you just heard this appeal. How about that?'

The reporters nodded dreamily. Most of them, those not actively necking each other, were still staring at Teesa and not really listening. The cameras, happily, seemed to know what to do.

As did the prick in the hat.

'So that's what this is all about, is it?' he said. Sweaty-faced, red-eyed, still flinging glances at the door. 'You're anti-corporate. This is a … what, a political thing?'

39

Myq lost a couple of candyfloss seconds trying to decide if he pitied or envied the man his exemption from Tee's spell, and only tuned back in when she stiffened beside him with an angry tut. He knew without waiting how it would go if he let her handle the Official Response, because it was the very same argument they'd had that morning.

Look, she'd snarled, unbuckling his clothes. *I don't give a damn about the corps and nor do you. We should just be honest about it. We want to … to break stuff. Right? To laugh and screw and scorch a trail. What's so bad about that? You think there has to be a meaning? There doesn't! You think we need a, what? A message? A bloody moral? We don't, Myq! All we need's to be alive and to smash and to run and run and never slow down, and I bet … I bet you, darling … I bet that's something everyone else wants too.*

This morning? He hadn't believed her. Didn't buy it. But then this morning she'd shortly thereafter done something with her mouth which had silenced all his objections. Which, alas, was unlikely to reoccur here. So he settled a calming hand on her shoulder, marvelling that he still had such presence of mind (just touching her made his cock stiffen and his brain turn to soup) and took a smart step forwards into the camera light.

'Yes,' he told the journo before Tee could speak. 'That's exactly it.'

People need a cause, he'd told her, before she'd got his pants off. *People want the explodo, yeah, fine. But they need to give themselves an excuse for it too.*

'It's about distribution of wealth,' he said. He'd practised this. 'In a federation of three hundred billion, 95% of the wealth is controlled by less than a million individuals. Almost all of them with ties to the megacorps which exist – supposedly – outside the sphere of political enga—'

'So you've got a beef with the superwealthy?'

Mike opened and shut his mouth a few times, monologue ruined.

'Y … yeah,' he stammered 'Yes, because w—'

'But aren't you Myquel Dobroba Pela-LeSire LeQuire? Former musical star from the Alliance territories?'

'Well … well, y—'

'By which I mean: weren't you more than a bit bloody rich yourself?'

Ohshit.

He'd known, of course, that sooner or later a positive ID would trickle down from the cops on Gateway. The prospect hadn't seemed to matter much in the run up: he'd known there was no going back, no return to Normal. Not since the instant Tee'd whispered *let's take the ship* that fateful morning after the jail.

But for it to happen so quickly? And to hear his name stated with such blunt indifference by an increasingly irritating little pustule in a hat?

'I … I've seen first-hand what financial unfairness looks like,' he invented madly. 'As you can see, I've turned my back on all that.'

'So how far does it go, Myq?' The journo dabbed absently at his forehead. 'You got a problem with *anyone* earning money? That it? Honest business people too?'

'Of course not. Only th—'

'So what if someone's worked hard all their life? Sweated blood. Let's say a … a trader. Built up a nice fortune as a result of their labours. You got a problem with him too? You want to go blow up his ship?'

'Look, I don't know who y—'

'A commodity baron, let's say. Someone in … *ohhh* … someone in the glander-trade.'

To his credit Myq sensed the trap before it yawned open, though not quickly enough to either understand or evade it. Teesa sucked in a breath and twitched beside him.

'Someone,' the journo said, 'like, let's pluck a name … someone like Madrien Axcelsus.'

'Who?' It rang a bell.

'Imperial businessman. Nice guy, by all accounts. Badly injured in his prime. Very sad. Only woke up recently.'

'What's this got to do w—'

'Apparently one of his indentured workers shot him in the spine and nicked his shuttle.'

Oh.

'Killed six other slaves on the way out.'

Ohhhhhhwait—

'Set fire to the whole place as she fled.'

You what?

The little man's beady eyes flicked sideways from Myq to Teesa.

'Is that the sort of wealth re-distribution you're about, oh noble social warriors?'

Myq realised as if dreaming, weirdly indignant that the man knew more about Tee than *he* did, that every single other journalist in the room was now ferociously engaged in removing clothes, rubbing and stroking and sweating and sucking with their eyes shut.

But not him. Not the guy in the hat.

Why not?

Only the cameras maintained a dispassionate overwatch, obediently autopanning back and forth between the bastard and his targets.

'Why are you really doing this, Teesa?' the little man hissed.

Teesa said *hah*.

Teesa shrugged, as if she'd known this whole stupid thing would fall apart.

Teesa fired a quiet smile at Myq, like: *at least we tried.*

And then withdrew the gun from her pocket.

'Freedom,' she said, simply.

'Very noble,' the man spat, sweating openly.

And at last it occurred to Myq that in every tremble and snarl, ever since his failed escape, the strange little journalist with the cam-lens above his eye had worn the bitter aspect of a man fully expecting to die. 'The noble psycho,' he sneered, 'who wants to set us all free.'

'You misunderstand,' Tee said. Giving him a strange look. 'I mean *my* freedom.'

Myq became uncomfortably aware his erection was almost certainly visible, at approximately the same instant Teesa primed the gun.

'Freedom to do exactly what the fuck I like.'

And she shot the journalist through the face.

They'd jumped five times, each in a random direction, pausing only to sunscoop extra fuel, before his heart began to slow down. He packed Tee into the bunk and fed her calmnarcs, guiltily claiming they were celebratory stimms, until she stopped whooping and relaxed enough for him to attach nullgee straps to hold her down. She'd fallen asleep after an hour of blissed-out mumbling.

For her own good, he told himself. *Heavy day.*

Her own good.

They'd run, of course. Left the little guy dead on the floor, hole through his head. Blood and brains and cauterised skin. Left the remainder of the journalistic pack grunting and salivating in orgiastic overload and made sure the nullsignal airlock was sealed behind them when they outcycled to freedom.

43

Still, it hadn't taken long for the feeds to go live. By the time Tee was asleep, when Myq slumped down at the liminals to go fishing through bandwidths it was clear the circus had been raging for hours already.

There they were: crystal-clear and bloody-bright on every newscast out, two lovers hunched over a body. He shouting purple panic. She howling venomous victory. Neither decipherable. And yeah, cut and spliced through it all, the highlights of the recorded show, ships smashing apart, account number, Tee's hands on hips, Myq's swagger, *'redistribution of wealth'*, moistened lips, *'Why are you really doing this, Teesa?'*

Why are *you really doing this, Tee?*

And the shot, and the blood. Over and over.

Phone-ins. Expert opinions. Senior cops vowing capture and conviction. Old band mates on low-width audio from half the galaxy away, claiming *we never liked him much anyway*. An endless, infinite wraparound slog of disgust and doom and impending justice.

And it wasn't until Myq switched it off with a cry, unable to bear one more Legal Expert, one more Representative of This/That Church, one more Horrified Joe Average, one more *anyone* spitting on his name, that he thought to check the balance in the account they'd set up.

Fifty-three-point-seven million creds, it read.

And there, below the readout, a list of donation reference-messages scrolled endlessly down one side.

keep it up

u guys r so nebular

amazingshowthnx

love you love your work

Very quietly, very quickly, Myquel took some drugs.

The tally had hit fifty-five mill before he could even crack open the stimmpack, and from the bed in the corner, drifting alone through who-knew-what fantastical places in her mind, Teesa made a sound a little like a sob and whispered:

'*Where are you? Please. Please. I've waited so long.*'

Even bombed off his overwrought tits, Myq was fairly sure she wasn't talking to him.

Four

The little man had barely changed since SixJen last saw him. Death notwithstanding.

Even the lens above his eye didn't seem out of place – a practical stand-in for the monoshot laser he'd worn when she first met him. 'Deathstare Dan' he'd called himself, without irony, presumably to the endless amusement of his piratical comrades. It was a name as cringeworthy as it was inaccurate: she doubted he'd ever actually used the stupid thing to lethal effect. Certainly on the day she'd first discovered him, all those years ago, shivering in the lavatory of the bifurcated *Holyhead*, his attempt to shoot her had succeeded only in scorching his own sub-trendy haircut.

He was, always had been, and in death remained, a loser beneath pity.

Only the blackened hole through the middle of his forehead, neatly cauterised when created but now puckered by morbid contraction and frost-haloed by its spell in the freezer, marked him apart from the cowardly reaver whose life she'd spared long ago. He'd been dead only two hours.

The *The* had arrived at Tun's Wart an infuriatingly short while after the *Shattergeist* hightailed into the warp. The clattering corridors of the station, mercifully insulated by the heavy walls of the morgue where she now stood, were still buzzing with excitement.

'That's him,' she monotoned at the mortician. 'Yes, indeed. That's my poor, poor brother.' She wouldn't have bothered trying to make it convincing even if she were capable of emoting, and the mortician simply nodded with the subservient couldn't-give-a-fuck-ness of a man already in receipt of a generous bribe.

'I expect you'll be wanting a moment alone,' he said.

She nodded. It was good when people knew the game.

She got started the moment he was gone. Pressing the edge of her habitually-carried flechette into the moulding of the camlens and, with a grunt of effort and a viscous slurp, prying it from the corpse's skull.

Poor little pirate, she thought. Trying to mean it.

It was strange though, this inanimate reunion. She hadn't thought of Dan, or of the *Holyhead* itself, in a long while. That bleak black monster had terrorised the exosystemic freight-lanes near Indaol for a half a decade already by the time she decided to go after it, and surely the years since – three? four? – were too few to justify her recollections becoming so foggy. Only an involuntary glance at the scars of her left arm marked the episode's relevance to her past.

Numb.

Numb in memory and mind.

The broad strokes of that great victory, at least, remained with her. At that time, she recalled, the hunt which to this day drove and consumed her had gone quiet, becalmed by a frustrating lack of information on the fugitive. No new glimmers of intel, no fresh sightings of the runner. Not for weeks. And as always during such lacunae she'd been deter-mined to stay busy, to hone the skills and accumulate the wealth that would, she knew, give her the edge whenever the Real Chase resumed.

It hadn't hurt that over the preceding year, while in pursuit of her prime target, she'd grown accustomed to hearing mention of the piratical *Holyhead* and its Captain, one Bradven Delino. So frequently had the dread vessel almost-but-not-quite crossed her path she'd become convinced it was somehow connected to her prey.

(Paranoia, she reflected, had been the last of her emotions to die.)

She'd spent a week at the oort cusp of the Indaol system, watching other mercs come and go. Each of them taking their doomed, dismal little shot at interstellar fame by picking a fight with Delino. She remembered him from the local Most Wanted vids as a disappointingly un-rakish man – the rumoured recipient of several letters of Marque from the Empire. It pleased some of the more senior Imperial senators, so the story went, to subsidise troublemakers near Federation space, and those pirates who bucked the swash-buckling trend in favour of pragmatism, hyperviolence and Actual Results were clearly the preferred agents of mischief.

Bradven Delino was the bigtime. He'd been, quite simply, SixJen's most triumphant kill, and she remained familiar enough with the terms of instinct and emotion to under-stand that the mere thought of him should've brought her both pride and pleasure. It didn't. She would've traded his scalp, she would've traded them *all*, for the luridly-dyed-in-pink-and-orange one that haunted her.

Teesa#32A[M/Tertius]

The runner.

Back in the morgue SixJen broke the strand of connec-tive gristle between Deathstare Dan's brain and the camera, lip curling at the sticky *snap*. For all her past exploits, all the tales and talents she'd accumulated during breaks in the primary hunt, she refused to let the trail go cold ever again. No more lacunae, no more pauses in pursuit. Not after coming so close last time. She unscrewed the camera's backplate, shaking out a treacly residue of neuroconductive exotics, and permitted her mind to wander backwards while she worked. The memories of those former glories, increasingly obscured though they were, would have to suffice.

So, yes: the fringes of Indaol. A week watching other bounty hunters being erased by Delino's outfit like salt in a hot spring. A second week sending an elaborate assortment of jury-rigged junkdrones and jalopies, each too pitiful to merit an assault, to drift through the dust-fields of the system where the *Holyhead* supposedly made its base. Sensors cranked high, remotely piloted at a safe distance.

She'd found Delino's base on the twelfth day. The thirteenth through eighteenth she simply watched the *Holyhead* come and go. Docking, repairs, departing on its raids. Every time it returned, after hours or days, with ammo spent and cargo pods brimming.

On the nineteenth day, five seconds after the monstrous thing breached back from hyperspace in its accustomed place, she'd flicked a switch inside the *The* and came as close to a sense of excited satisfaction as she ever had.

That part, obscenely, was the fuzziest memory of all.

The *Holyhead* struck realspace and ploughed into the mines she'd laid. The ripple of plasma that consumed the vessel took out most of its shields and half its turrets. The now-superfluous drones she'd been using, hastily retrofitted with unstable cores, kamikazed cheerfully into its flanks and accounted for the rest. By which time the EM-generators she'd painstakingly mounted on three local asteroids, each rock slightly greater than a mile across, had accumulated sufficient momentum to shove their colossal cargoes out of the oort-field and, one by one, into their targets.

Two had utterly erased the pirates' base from the moonlet where it was lodged. The ops there hadn't even had time to dispatch fighters to aid Delino, and SixJen was cautiously confident she could *just* remember the startled comm-shrieks on the wire as the mountainbombs struck.

The *Holyhead*, all but defenceless, was messily severed in two by the third monolith.

Thinking back now, she figured it'd taken about a day to wander through the wreck in search of the Captain. Some parts had clumsily autosealed against the vacuum, so she'd been obligated to schlep through fractured decks with pistol in hand, ungainly in her RemLok suit, killing those worth killing, collecting IDs on those bearing bounties. (That, she guessed, had probably been the part she'd enjoyed the most. It was difficult to say.)

She'd found Delino half dead in his cabin, in a section of the hulk still sealed from the void. A suite of rooms without personal effect or affectation; Spartan and spotless. She'd known, then, what he was.

But she'd said the word anyway, just to be sure. And he'd looked her in the eye and nodded. Said it back. And then she'd killed him.

And this – *This* – was the part she remembered most clearly.

Standing over him, as his weightless blood formed a grim coriolis, as she'd unbuckled the arm of her suit to calmly slice a fresh scar into her left arm – *number seven* – she'd contemplated the man's approach to the obsession they shared. Shared, in fact, with all twelve of their brothers: those alive and those dead.

It was impressive, she'd decided. Throughout the whole of the great hunt which defined her she'd elected to seek the prey alone, deadly and determined, without companion or confederate. Her game, her rules, her cunning. But this man Delino? He'd raised a small army. He'd founded an enclave. He'd stretched forth his resources with far greater daring.

It'd got him killed in the end, but still.

Something, she remembered muttering, *to think about*.

On the way back to the *The* she'd found 'Deathstare' Dan hiding in the shitter. Once he'd got the tedious business of self-defence out the way, hair-eradicating skull-implanted lasershot and all, she'd given him a calculating glare and made up her mind.

'You're coming with me,' she'd said.

Back in the now the mortician poked his head round the door.

'You nearly done?' he grumbled to the frozen air. 'Only they'll be wanting a report, and if h—'

'Piss off or I'll shoot you in the crotch.'

'Rightio.'

She finished removing the datachips from the camlens interior and crammed it messily back into the socket. And spared a final glance for the face of 'Deathstare' Dan Megrith. Minion #1.

'New life,' she'd told him, the day she cut him loose. 'New name. My gifts to you.'

'Wh-wh-what's the catch?'

She'd smiled. This was back when that was still a thing she sometimes did.

'Constant vigilance.'

She'd told him what to look out for. She'd named the prey. She'd provided the strange and senseless human '*who*', though of course had said nothing of the '*why*'. She'd given him a tiny iron clip, a magnetised earring he was instructed to wear at all times. 'To stop the runner,' she'd said, tapping her head, 'from making you hers. To make you immune.' She'd suggested he take work as an info-narc, a cop, a crim, a journalist. Someone, anyway, with big ears. She'd told him she'd implanted an extremely expensive micro-beacon into his snazzy new livestreaming biocamera, and she'd told him it would unfailingly auto-ping the *The* in the event of its removal. Or of his death. Or, critically, of him whistling aloud a specific little ditty, which she then proceeded to teach him.

(*He managed two out of three*, she thought. *Not bad, Deathstare Dan.*) But for the nullzone of the whispering room she might even have received the message in time.

In the years since engaging the man's service she'd accumulated – at last count – a total of twenty-one patsies under similar circumstances. Twenty, now.

Favours owed. Fears displaced. Lives extended unexpectedly.

'Teesa,' she told them all. 'Teesa #32A[M/Tertius]. Formerly owned by Madrien Axcelsus.'

They nodded. They repeated it back. Every time. They sweated and willed her to leave them alone, to go away. Each one of them, she was sure, was convinced she was insane.

'Find her,' she'd told them. 'Find her and every cred I've ever earned is yours.'

(Some of them, she liked to think, believed her. She'd meant it.)

'But let her get away …' She meant this part too. 'I will come for you.'

In the morgue she slipped the data-chip into a pocket and headed for the door.

Deathstare Dan, at the very least, had spared her the trouble.

An hour out from the station, watching the camlens footage for the fifth time, SixJen chewed mechanically at a nutripack and wondered if it was supposed to taste of anything. Above

52

her, as broad and invasively close as the *The*'s imagers could manage, Teesa #32A stared directly at her, hollow snout of her pistol yawning black, and said: *the freedom to do exactly what the fuck I like.*

A flash. A noise. And the footage looping back to the start.

'You ask me,' Lex chirped, adopting a tone SixJen had long ago learned to recognise as his Cautious Bullshittery voice, 'she has sad eyes.'

('Bullshittery', that is, because of course he – *it* – had no more capacity for understanding the notion of 'sad' than any other electrical puzzlebox mimicking empathy. Particularly when perceived in the magical emo-twinkles of a psychopath's vid-recorded eyes.)

(And 'Cautious' because, *well—*)

'I *didn't* ask, Lex.'

'No, but—'

'So shut up.'

'Right.'

She finished the nutripack in silence. That had been down to Lex too – a diplomatic reminder, a few minutes earlier, that she hadn't eaten anything for a day. Watching the footage through again now, while chewing, SixJen told herself it was for precisely that type of practical organisa-tion – *eat, sleep, crap* – that she kept Lex around. Of course one didn't have to be a genius, let alone a microscale supercomputer, to figure out the same duties could've been handled by a less … *well—*

Eccentric? Opinionated? Annoying?

—a less *human-seeming* companion.

But still, but still. Even with a double emphasis on the 'seeming' part of *human-seeming*, even with Lex's shrill idio-syncrasies being no more than impersonations codified by his manufacturers, still the suspicion troubled SixJen that she tolerated him due to some deep-rooted need for human contact, ersatz or otherwise.

The Voight-Comal C-902 Personal Companion, after all, nicknamed the 'Culex' for its mosquitolike size and voice, was designed for the sorts of lonely nobodies for whom an abrasively needy gadget might constitute perfect company. (He probably had a vibrate setting, though she'd never asked.) At root, Lex represented an aggravating, infuriating little pet – an entity dichotomously programmed to be submissively *owned* and yet aggressively challenging all at once.

And so the real truth? The truth which she always seemed to recall at times just like this, then studiously forgot for the sake of her own sanity, was that even though he could be deconstructed to a bundle of metals and quantum charges, even though he was non-sentient and unremarkable, Lex was still more innately attuned to humanity than she was.

More alive than she was.

Sometimes that came in handy. *Sad eyes*, he'd said. *She has sad eyes.* SixJen hadn't even thought to look.

She switched off the feed and drummed fingers against the controls. Finished chewing her last bland mouthful of nutripack. And then, as if unable to bear the gloom and silence (though in truth simply averse to inaction), went back to roaming through the reams of stellar reportage she'd already guzzled and dismissed during the journey to the Tun/Ton system.

The media condemnations continued apace. If such a thing were possible they seemed now even more abject, more shrill, than before. The footage looped on and on: ships crumbling, lovers talking, lasers firing, journos fucking.

(Expert Opinion, incidentally, had reached consensus in the hypothesis that the fugitives must have released a sex drug into the air of the conference room to cause such extremes of indignity and indecency amongst blameless members of the journalistic community; and hence had added chemical assault to their numberless crimes.)

Yet a countersignal was growing too. A backwash of honest opinion which troubled SixJen far more deeply, at some not-quite-understood remove.

They were youngsters, mostly. Kids secretly phoning the microwave shows while their parents slept – to confess they'd donated their pocket creds, their allowances, their savings (and in one giggling girl's case the contents of her dad's retirement fund), in the ungainly name of Destructertainment. On another channel, a lank-haired poetry star, fashionably androgynous and openly bombed on something which had turned the whites of hisher eyes a brackish green, cawed and honked through a specially-improvised piece called *Free To Destroy*. The commentary feeds of every two-bit journal on the local net spumed illiterate scrolltrolls word-wanking over 'Tasty Teesa'. Inevitably-named 'Tee-shirts' had already infected the designer sites, and even the pomp-cliques and culturecrits of the artshows had found a way – '*inspirational living-installation*'; '*neo-po-mo expression of retrogressive (and hence, ahaw, progressive!) nu-nihilism*'; '*sub-subversive manifestation of the kitsch brutalist enlightenment!*' – to transform the gratuitous into the germane.

SixJen sighed. The runner danced through the limelight with a smirk – *sad eyes, sad eyes* – and she, the hunter, prowled and paced the shadows. Uncertain.

Most worrying of all, in that it escalated the phenomenon from the merely unfamiliar to the actively obstructive, a series of false positives had invaded the usual space-lane

55

mediocrity of the newsies. In a community as bogglingly vast as the Federation, ships and crews were forever disappearing and dying, but whereas such materiel losses were usually the preserve of the bottom-of-screen tickertape, or the thinbeam digest pages, now every fresh shipping incident was blared with klaxons wailing and anchormen howling.

Is it them? Is this their next attack?

SixJen switched it off, yet again, in disgust.

'People,' said Lex, characteristically forgetting his instruction of silence and unaware he was parroting the very revelation, in the mind of Myquel Dobroba Pela-LeSire LeQuire, which had engendered the whole carnival, 'really like watching shit blow up.'

SixJen slumped against her geestraps and brooded.

She'd hoped, without much enthusiasm, that Dan's eyefeed might supply a clue. Some quiet, intangible something (*she has sad eyes, she has sad eyes*) lost amidst the spectacle and impersonality of the other newsfeeds from that conference room. Something to give her an edge, to keep her in contention, to show her the tracks in the sand.

An edge. That, she'd learned again and again, was often all it came down to. The minutiae. The endless hours of thought and preparation.

After all, how else was she supposed to fill the dead hours?

A man-eating tiger leaves footprints through the forest. A Merovingian apex-crab leaves a slick of hydrogenous pheromones through the swamp. Even a Ford-cluster Megalodon, void-born and void-borne, can be traced from the fucking glandular miniwarps it shits out while feeding.

But the runner?

(She dug a hand in a pocket and fished out the sharp little flechette. Aware but not caring enough to stop. Not feeling the first cut.)

56

The runner could smash and shatter all she pleased. She could jut up her head and proclaim herself. She could strut and preen in the hunter's glare——

——and then vanish without trace.

Fucking faster-than-light travel!

The chase – the fight – was never meant to be like this.

SixJen switched the stolen eyefeed back on and silently dared Lex to comment. He had better sense.

'… all above board,' Deathstare Dan was saying, now for the sixth time, his view favouring the boy. 'Someone in … *ohhh* … someone in the glander-trade.' For the sixth time Teesa hissed as if slapped. 'Someone like, let's pluck a name … someone like Madrien Axcelsus.'

The pop star boyfriend scowled, out of his depth. 'Wh … who?'

'Imperial businessman. Nice guy, by all accounts. Badly injured in his prime. Very sad. Only woke up recently.'

Watching, self-cutting, SixJen was on the verge of permitting herself a tiny sliver of mental pride aimed at poor dead Dan – specifically at his impressive provocation of the fugitives, presumably in an attempt to avoid the whole 'if you let her get away I will hunt you down' part of their agreement – when she saw it.

Sad eyes. Sad eyes.

Except they weren't. Not in that moment.

Throughout the whole thing, the whole journo-haranguing-an-unprepared-celeb routine, Teesa's face had remained clouded. Shuttered down, dreamlike, and – *yes, okay, fine* – sad. Sad like a memory. Sad like a moment's unexpected recall. Sad (and here SixJen was making calculations based on emotions and expressions she could barely remember) like someone reliving something painful for the first time in a long time.

She'd forgotten.

57

Madrien Axcelsus. The fire. The other slaves, the fat man stumbling and bleeding …

Deathstare Dan had reminded her of a life she didn't even know she'd had.

And as the woman remembered …? As the name of the slave-owner she'd escaped from, the man she'd nearly killed in the act, as his name infiltrated the runner's crazy brain and set fires in the edges of her mouth, those eyes – *sad*, ha! *Sad fucking eyes, but not for long!* – they changed. Even SixJen could see it.

Teesa's sadness went away.

Her eyes rolled towards the camera. And lit up, for a fraction, above a smile so ghastly that, had SixJen not seen it herself, she would've doubted the capacity of a face so sweet to bear it.

Around the girl the drama hazed on. The boy blurting questions, the journalist demanding motives. *Why are you really doing this, Teesa?*

But the runner's eyes stayed on the camera. Like a secret message. Like divine communion between prey and predator.

Come and get me.

SixJen gaped as if slapped. Marvelled, for a second, at the depth of emotion still locked up inside her; at her own capability to feel.

Madrien Axcelsus.

She's remembered him.

He's the key.

And SixJen flicked off the feed for the sixth and final time and nodded to herself.

'I know where they're going,' she said.

'Eh?' Lex sounded doubtful. 'How's that?'

'Because she wants to be caught.'

Five

This time: war drums.

This time an aggressively actuated beat, pounding between synthesised guitar shrieks and throbbing along helter-skelter melodies. It sped with every acceleration of the *Shattergeist*, dived with every manoeuvre, roared with every flare on the scanner.

Smartmusic software: innovative audio solutions attuned to the *Shattergeist*'s systems, like a Soundtrack To Your Day™.

It'd cost a bloody fortune, and Myq was uncomfortably aware it was significantly better than his old band had ever been. It was giving him a headache all the same.

One of the cargo runners, he noticed, was still shooting at them. It limped grimly across the scanner, surrounded by the broken wrecks of five matching craft killed just before, spattering its ammo with one remaining pod. Brave but stupid.

Luckily for its pilot Teesa didn't seem in any rush to finish it off. Alas, nor did she seem especially interested in avoiding its gunfire. Myq bit down on the naggish 'Watch out!' rising in his throat, bored of being the Sensible One, and rubbed his temples.

B-dum, b-dum, b-dum.

Ignoring the tracerfire entirely (either trusting to the *Shattergeist*'s shields or simply not caring), Tee coiled the ship up and round to blast full pelt towards yet another of the wriggling shibboletti spore-cows dangling in space, giggling as she went. Hundreds of the rotund creatures were bobbing, wobbling and flexing round the debris zone, spilled free from the cargo pods that had been transporting them.

'Heeeeeeeeeere it coooooomes!'

She'd noticed early on, hours before, how satisfyingly the shibboletti popped if you crashed into them. She'd been obsessively repeating the act ever since, like a kid determined to burst every balloon at the party. The music software intuited a rising drum roll as they homed in, then—

Cymbal crash! Guitar solo!

—the creature splashed apart like a jewelled beach ball, eyeless head flapping, gaseous bulk spraying frothy green powders across the ship's flaring shields. Teesa squealed with glee.

'Your turn!' she yelled, dragging Myq to the console. 'Your turn!'

He took the liminals clumsily, powerless in the face of her enthusiasm, and brought the ship about. Far off to starboard the crippled freighter, like some gouty octogenarian trying to keep up with a crazed grandchild, swivelled awkwardly and kept on firing. Fresh shibboletti kept spilling from the cavity where its pods had been before it'd run afoul of the *Shattergeist*. There seemed to be a never-ending supply of the poor, bloated brutes.

This, Myq thought, *could take a while.*

Curiously the musical software had decided the appropriate sound for each ammo-strike against their shields was a flatulent tuba honk, so his assumption of the controls was marked by an embarrassing medley of dissonant farts as lead rattled around them. It felt like a personal slight against his piloting.

'Can we turn that bloody thing off?' he muttered, as the drums started up again.

60

'There!' Teesa cried, ignoring him. 'Look at the size of *that* one!'

It was, indeed, a whopper. Myq obediently accelerated, trying to sigh as if weary but, in fact, feeling his heart race. Infected, as ever, by Teesa's influence.

The shibboletti were among the galaxy's stranger forms of wildlife. Roughly spherical, on closer inspection they were formed of two lobed halves like cloves of garlic with a stalk-protrusion for a head (pocked by damp osmosis patches and rudimentary sense organs) and a set of innumerable wormlike 'feet' with which they could blindly stumble about. Like much of the non-terrestrial life encountered over the millennia the shibboletti defied neat categorisation as 'animals', bearing more in common with spore-releasing fungi. The honking things were farmed on the independent world of Shibboleth for which they were named, which was itself so-called (so the story went) because of its occupants' bloody-minded insistence on manufacturing a bizarre accent just to make outsiders uncomfortable about pronouncing things wrong.

All of this Myq had swiftly gleaned from a netsearch during Teesa's beastie-bursting shenanigans, all while trying to ignore the music, and as he now powered towards the huge specimen ahead he quietly wished he'd had the chance to find out whether they were capable of feeling pain or not.

Not, he supposed, that it would've made any difference. Somewhere off beyond the field of bleating and blustering creatures, and the tumbling hulks of the cargo ships which had been transporting them, a small flotilla of media vessels lurked voyeuristically.

The galaxy's watching.
Gotta give 'em a show.

61

It was Teesa who'd brought them here, of course. A nondescript patch of space at the gravity well limits of #A5FFP – a planetless star with an unfussy blue/green sheen.

'You'll see,' she kept saying. 'You'll see.' He'd assumed she had some prior knowledge about a likely target for their ongoing rampage (though he couldn't imagine where she'd picked up such a tip) and he wasn't wrong. #A5FFP, it transpired, was the preferred hop point for freighters on the cargo run between Shibboleth and the big trading outposts on the edge of the territory. Five or six FTL jumps into the ride, the livestock haulers would pause above the petroleum maelstroms of the grimy sun's surface to recalculate nav solutions, slurp on some hasty coffee and enjoy a moment's peace.

Then get blown to hell by a pair of insane crowdfunded sex-crazed lunatics – all in time to over-bassed music – while an impartial gallery of journalists looked on. So far the honourable newshounds had elected not to summon the authorities, presumably preferring to wait for each new cargo ship to come stumbling to its (photogenic) doom – and recording the *'Geist* whimsically exploding shibboletti in the interim. It was, Myq grudgingly supposed, great TV.

The money in their account had never poured in so fast.

The drum roll began again. The great creature loomed huge onscreen, blissfully unaware – *NoGod, I hope so* – of the ionic fistfront descending towards it. But at the last instant its idiot writhings ejected a wisp of powdery gas from some unseen orifice, propelling it halfway clear, so the *'Geist* tore inelegantly through its side instead of performing a perfect strike. No cymbal crash for Myq, no crazed guitar solo, just the comedy scales of a swanee whistle and a protracted raspberry as the startled creature corkscrewed off in a long spastic stream, like an untied balloon.

'I don't think this music thing likes me,' Myq grumbled, gesturing Tee to take back the controls. But instead of sliding the liminals towards herself she simply slipped onto his lap and wrapped her hands round his, pinning them to the stick, then executed a few impetuous barrel rolls while wriggling. Bored, he supposed, of killing pseudocows.

'How much do you know,' she said, turning up the music, 'about life cycles?'

'You what?'

'You know … egg laying, larval stages, all that.'

'Can't say I'm much of an expert.' He squinted at the side of her face. Her voice sounded weird. 'Why?'

'Interesting subject.' She jiggled gently against his crotch – a silent titter, a private joke. Then steered the *'Geist* slowly, inexorably, towards the half-dead cargo ship, still gamely firing at them.

The media vessels, Myq noticed, were gently shunting forwards. Sensing, he supposed, something special.

'I mean, it's not always just a case of … ha, of When Mummy and Daddy Love Each Other Very Much. Mammals are pretty fucking dull, comparatively speaking.'

'What's got into you?'

The cargo ship hosed a stream of ordnance against their shields. Freshly tuned and powered-up for the tenth time – the fruits of numberless donations – they barely registered the tickle of lead. The software, Myq noted glumly, was still cheerfully associating the salvo with fart sounds.

Tee didn't seem to mind. In fact, Tee didn't seem to be paying attention to much of anything except her own words.

'Even terra life, you know? Plenty of weirdness there. Insects spend most of their lives as grubs. And young crustaceans are just these … these blobby little plankton things for months before they get all crusty and clawy. And as for sex? Ha! Fish don't fuck, poor things, just squirt their junk all over the place and mix it up. Most birds – did you know this? Most birds don't even have cocks or cracks. Just these slimy patch things.'

'Tee, you're … you're kind of freaking me out. Why do you know all this? And what's it got to do w—' Myq stopped. Blinked. The music, as if psychically reactive, affected a long descending whistle tone, like a bomb falling into his brain.

Oh no …

Teesa half turned to face him, a quizzical smile on her face. 'What is it?'

He cleared his throat. 'Are you … are you trying to suggest we have a kid?'

She just threw back her head and roared with laughter.

'Just checking,' he muttered.

The *Shattergeist* now hung a scant few kliks from the cargo ship. The squat thing, entirely wrecked along one flank, had nosed its way protectively into the field of debris round the even-more-successfully-buggered corpses of its fellows. Some of the crews from the other ships had bailed in time: the scanner now finding them gathered in a frightened little cluster of RemLok suits just behind the surviving vessel.

Which, as if intuiting that the predator responsible was finally intending to finish the job, finally gave up on its pointless firing.

Teesa tapped a control – *weapons hot … here we go … –* and picked up on her monologue as if it was never interrupted.

'*Non*-terrestrial life – *now*. Soooo much weirdness. You've got your supra-binary life forms, first of all. Three genders, four, even five. Different combinations of parenthood, different outcomes for different environmental situations. You've got your novel life forms which reproduce through, what, through consumption or decomposition or bloody parasitic possession. And that's before you get to the trippy aphysical stuff. You know there's a thing out in the Frelix system that spends two thirds of its life as a drifting chain of pheromones? And now they think – "*they*", y'know? The experts – they think we're going to start recognising a lot of humdrum stuff as exotic higher-plane life. Piece of music that won't get out of your head? Madcap idea you've just got to spread around? What's that if not reproduction?'

Myq gurgled.

He, throughout all of this, was having something of a crisis. For the first time he could remember, since meeting Teesa, despite being neither exhausted nor sore, and despite the more-than-conspicuous wriggling of her arse against his lap, he did not have an erection.

'You … Tee, you said you were a chauffeur, right? Back when you were … y'know?'

'A slave.'

'Yeah. So. Not a biology teacher?'

Another half turn to face him, another sideways smile, another bum-squirm. Another profound failure to arouse. 'Long time ago,' she said. 'Learnt a lot since then. Lot of water under the bridge.'

Right, he thought. *Yeah.*

Like that bit about how you crippled your boss and set fire to the whole place.

Water. Bridge.

He hadn't summoned the courage to ask her about that yet. Partly, he supposed, it felt like such a petty thing to quibble over, in context.

Like: *Hey Tee, y'know how we spend most days exploding stuff? How we've probably racked up a double-nebular body count? How you shot a guy in the face back in Tun/Ton? Okay, well, just so's you know, all that pales into comparison to you Not Telling Me about a significantly-less-horrible episode from your distant past.*

Whiny crap.

Here was the truth: Teesa wasn't *his*. Wasn't anyone's. Someone like her never would be, never could be, never should be. Myq felt stupid and childish for even being hurt at the lack of disclosure; rendered a whingeing brat by his unthinking need to understand and know her fully.

I love her. NoGod help me, I love her.

I want every part of her. Memories and all.

Teesa ripped the cargo ship apart with supreme indifference. The music software barely seemed to respond, sensitive to her ambivalence. She spared, Myq noticed, a perfectly aimed shot for a single smallish shibboletti tumbling past, which burst in a satisfying haze of spores.

'Take those things,' she said, nodding at the twist of fur and skin which remained of the creature, inured to the operatic curtains of nuclear fire blossoming nearby. 'They're barely conscious, they're just as happy in a vacuum as atmosphere, they're totally inedible, they're extremely ugly, but they have one of the most exciting reproductive cycles you'll ever hear about.'

'Uh, Tee …?' Myq said. She'd softly started guiding the '*Geist* into the flaming debris. 'What're y—'

'What happens is, they're all female. Every single one. Grow up from spores, see? Airborne – tiny little things. Settle on a bit of plant matter, om-nom-nom, few years later you've got your basic shaggy shibboletti. And they're very valuable. I mean, that's exactly the point. Somewhere down in those ballbag skins there's a clutch of drippy little glands that make some of the finest narcotics known to man. Illegal in the Federation, but in the Empire? Or some quaint little indie-world? These beasties're worth a bomb, Myq.'

She smirked at that. Like sharing a joke with herself.

As if dreaming, Myq watched lumps of wreckage and great green tangles of dead shibboletti carom off the shields. She drove them deeper into the morass, searching, so it seemed, for something. But beneath his confusion at her plans, beneath his bewilderment at her weird ejaculation of expertise, beneath even his growing panic at the startling lack of horniness crackling between them, Myq felt a tiny spark of memory light up in his mind.

A commodity baron, a wheedling little voice said. *Someone in ... ohhh ... someone in the glander-trade.*

The reporter. The dead reporter had said that.

'Tee,' Myq said. 'Tee, how d'you know so much about shibbole—'

'Now here's the fascinating part. If you get enough of the damn things together, all at once, one of them starts to change. Takes a week or two. Becomes ... well, for want of a better word: male.'

'Your owner ... back when you were a sl—'

'Sssh, listen.' She banked right, nudging aside a sheet of dented hull. Checking, so Myq thought, to make sure the media ships were close at hand. 'Now, the gland-merchants? The farmers? It's in their interest not to let this happen. I'll come back to that. So they regulate it really carefully these days. They've got, ohhh, sprays, hormone-mists, all that. Make sure no males appear. They let it happen once in a blue moon, sure, but only under really carefully controlled conditions. It's this whole big thing.'

'Tee, where are ... you ... taking ...'

His voice died. The music went sinister.

Ohhhhno.

Hanging ahead of them, swivelling comically to face the '*Geist* with suit-controlled airbursters puffing, the ejected crewmen of all those ships dangled in the void. Clustered together.

Safety – so they'd thought – in numbers.

'Why don't the farmers want males popping up?' She gripped his hands round the stick, holding them in place. 'I'll tell you. It's because when a male's mature – all big and bristly and red – he honks out this great cloud of hormones. *Poooft!* And the second that happens? All those hundreds and thousands of big farty females, Myq, they get oh-so-very frisky.'

She – and hence *he* – pressed forwards on the stick. The cluster of figures began to writhe in panic. The music did something shivery and abstract, building in shrill tones.

'Tee … Tee, the journos're watching.'

'You know what a frisky shibboletti female does, Myq?'

The crewmen flopping, thrashing, shoving at one another, trying to beat physics. Trying to soar free of the pack. The music spiralling high …

'They're *watching*, Tee. Exploding shit – fine! People *like* that, but—'

'Exploding shit. Ha! Exploding shit! You're so right!'

'What? I don't … Tee, there are limits, okay, and—'

'A frisky shibboletti gets unstable, Myq. One little knock? *Boom*! System floods with unstable organics. Literally detonates. One after another, *chain reaction* right through the herd. Boom! Boom! Boom! Blasts unfertilised spores right across the sky!'

'Tee, don't, don't, don't—'

He tried to pry her free, tried to turn the ship, tried to do *anything*, but with a strength belying her slight frame she clung to his hands, rushing forwards, crushing them both into the geecouch, grim smile spreading. She crept a single finger out from the stick to stab at a control.

[SHIELDS LOWERED.]

'What the f—?'

'The male's the last one to pop. Fertilises as many of those spores as it can. Great whacking clouds of the things. Can you imagine?'

'Teeeeee—'

'Lovemaking, Myq. The act of lovemaking.' The music spiked. The crewmen thrashed. 'Making love through destruction.'

And the crewmen splattered against their armour, and the music roared and spun and crashed, and the media ships inched forwards to lap it all up, and bodies spumed and decompressed and went brittle, and Myq said *nononono*, and something that might've been a head got lodged in the brackets of the scan-arrays until it froze and clunked away, and it wasn't until Tee was ducking and racing free of the debris, thumbing the FTL to who-knew-where, that he realised with jaw agape that whatever monomaniacal little spell had come over her had passed, that her whooping and howling glee was back with a vengeance, and that – in simple consequence – his erection had instantly returned.

'Fun,' she said, jiggling, as they hit warpspace.

The media ships followed. Well-trained weasels, they slipped along cosmic tunnels in pursuit of the *Shattergeist*'s signature exotics, hot on their heels for each of the five jumps they took, maintaining during stopovers the safe distance of jackals watching a lionkill. At one point Teesa muttered something abstruse about them already overstaying their welcome.

Myq said nothing about that. He had bigger things in mind.

'Why did you have to do that?' he kept saying. 'They were … those were *real people*.'

69

'By which you mean you could see them instead of them being inside ships. It's no different, silly boy.'

He gaped a bit at that. Another hop. Another crash from hyperspace.

'Where are we going?' he started up again. 'Why did you have to …? Those. Those bloody reporters, look. Shouldn't we try to lose them? Tee, why did you do that? *What's going on?*'

And so on.

'You'll see,' she kept saying. Peeling off her clothes. Peeling off his. 'You'll see.'

'But. Why did you *do* that? Why did you have to tha—?'

'I didn't have to, Myq.' Was that a flicker of irritation he saw, deep in her eyes? 'I didn't have to, but I did. That's sort of the point, darling.'

On one of the stopovers, when his self-conscious worrying evidently overcame her predilection for enigma, she shot him a carefully-rehearsed *get ready to be wrong* look, logged into the remote-access bank, and waved for his attention.

Donations tumbled in faster than the system could track.

'See?' she said.

There aren't any limits.

And then the last hop. The stars settling to static. A cloudy green planet rotating below. And Tee smirking at him, both still sweaty from the last bout.

'Shibboleth,' she said.

A commodity baron, Myq remembered. *Someone in … ohhh … someone in the glander-trade.*

Apparently one of his indentured workers shot him in the spine and nicked his shuttle.

70

The questions were already rising in his chest when Tee interrupted them with a great yelp of joy and the music, still infuriatingly loud, ear-raped with a blast of crazy.

Alarms, lights, fiery flares and missile contrails.

[ALERT: MULTIPLE FIRING-SOLUTIONS DETECTED.]

The cops were waiting.

Six

'All right,' SixJen said. 'It's them.'

The cops – *the idiots* – began to whoop and cheer down the radio. She should've expected that. She might even have excused it, coming as it did from a pair of action-starved provincial flyboys so hopped on stimms and AggroUps it was a miracle they didn't get into a fight every time they passed a mirror, if they hadn't both blundered one step further into the realms of dickwitted overexcitement by instantaneously firing off their missiles.

Idiots.

In all their paranoid tightfistedness, and with a neurotic refusal to give credence to the insights of a mere mercenary, the top brass at Shibboleth's semi-privatised no-bit LawCom had assigned a meagre two ships to assist in SixJen's orbital vigil. Even when she'd taken a passable stab at feigning incandescence towards the precinct commander – *don't you know who I'm talking about? They're coming* here, *you sticky little mistake!* – the man conceded only one extra ship, and no extra pilot.

'Dunyer wreck it neither,' he'd warned, waggling a finger.

She was grouchily grateful for that, at least. She'd decided she couldn't field the *The* directly against the *Shattergeist*, not now the runner knew its shape and ident. One glance at SixJen's pride and joy (as it were) on the edge of a firefight and that psychotic little witch could be sure to—

To what?

Run a mile? Hit FTL and not look back? Turn and bring the fight?

Or reveal she'd been expecting it all along and unveil her master plan?

(The runner's not supposed to bloody scheme!)

None of those outcomes accorded with SixJen's preferred species of victory anyway – both achieving *and* surviving it all at once. So an honorary cop she'd have to temporarily be. The commander's skinflintery, alas, had gone further still.

''Arfload of ammo's all yer having,' he'd burbled, thicker than his own accent. 'Dun*know*yer, dun*trust*yer, dun*like*yer. An whyth fuck wouldey fugertives com*ere* hennywise? You earda 'casts. Theyoff aving funs 'sploding freighters in the oo-knows-where. Caught my'sown fucking daughter dernating to ther bankyccount, other day.'

The newscasts had indeed trickled through. It was perhaps illustrative that even here, on a frontier farmworld so independent it had manufactured its own accent – even *here* all the buzz was of the *Shattergeist* and its nihilistic adventures. Infuriatingly, there'd been no video received yet of its most recent predations, and the vox-reporters were still being vague about the 'where'. If SixJen had been a cynic (she was) she might have guessed (she did) that the hacks were being deliberately circumspect about the places they were called to, in order to keep the Feds from showing up to spoil the fun. But the fact remained: the *Shattergeist* had occupied itself the past few days ripping holes in cargo freighters before committing an act of calculated murder so gratuitous that the on air outrage-spouters could barely line up fast enough to decry it.

No shields.

Eight ejected pilots. Hit-and-run. No shields.

She wanted to feel the crunch.

And the donations? They just kept on coming.

SixJen had tried to explain to the commander her hunch, tried to illustrate why the *Shattergeist* would, she was sure, turn eventually towards Shibboleth; even tried to persuade him that the 'unfortunate cargo ships' in the carefully-edited vox-reports were quite possibly the very ones which had been setting off from his homeworld all week …

But her explanations sounded frail and speculative even before she'd said them, plus she dared not risk her insight being spread around – *my kill, my kill, nobody else's*. So she'd waved it all away mid-argument, swallowed the jagged pills of Only Three Ships with stony-faced grace, and got the fuck on with Waiting In Orbit.

'Yuz got thraydays,' the Commander'd said as she left.

SixJen wasn't the type to generalise along ethnic lines – she distributed her apathy towards the living with politic equality – but as the missiles fired by her new comrades snaked into the void she mused that it didn't reflect well on the people of Shibboleth that the two police pilots appeared even denser than their boss.

'Firecrackaway!' one whooped.

'Foxwun, foxwun!' cried the other.

She was beginning to wish she hadn't involved the locals at all.

'Scanners got the confirm on the target,' Lex chirped, his voice an unlikely relief in the tight confines of the borrowed copship. 'It's definitely them. Tweedledum's missile goes kablooey in forty-two, Tweedledee's in forty-four.'

Those idiots.

The runner, the prey – *sad eyes, sad eyes* – had appeared at the edge of the Shibboleth cluster with all the arrogant swagger SixJen had been expecting: the pimped-out yacht

all but screaming its ident. The copships (all Vipers, all
decked out in LookatMe reds and blues, fellow pilots barking
yokel machismo), had let slip their smartkillers the second
the scanners pinged. Two contrails of dispersing soot and
radiated heat.

'I told you,' she monotoned into the comm, wishing she
still had it in her to snarl, 'to wait for my mark.'

The men 'pffft'd' predictably, resuming their steroidal
pigshit. 'Yerl still get y'money!' she made out, as if that
settled it.

That's what mercenaries want, right?

'Thirty and thirty-two seconds,' Lex said.

'Any reaction?'

'Not a peep. Target's just chilling. Probably too busy
biffing in there. You think they even know what's coming?'

'They know.' *They'd better.*

Strangely enough SixJen's irritation, which existed in the
abstract sense that she should be feeling it but couldn't, was
not predicated purely on the risk of being robbed of her
kill. Oh, naturally that was an element: she'd taken pains
to arrange the limits of her cooperation with the cops and
had spent literally hours out here with Dim and Dimmer
twiddling thumbs, double checking they understood the
same.

Reason to suspect visitors of interest en route—

In exchange for ident and tactical intel I demand the following rights—

No action until my say-so—

Here to support me, not vice-versa—

Do not *fire unless—*

Etcetera etcetera.

'Maybe it's your winning way with people,' Lex muttered,
as the missiles jinked into final-approach vectors. She went
to give the casing of his little button body a punitive flick

– old habit – and only remembered he wasn't there when she jabbed herself instead. She wondered if she would've smiled about that, once.

'Sorry,' he said anyway.

Watching from afar.

No, kill theft wasn't the big fear. She'd seen the *Shattergeist* fly. She knew a couple of farmcops in median-spec Vipers weren't about to filch her holy moment.

'Eighteen and twenty seconds.'

Rather it was a simple matter of technical knowhow. Smartmissiles could be relied upon to grimly pursue targets only in the absence of obfuscatory radar returns. It followed that the one and only time a halfway decent pilot *really* didn't want to be shooting his load early, and offloading his tactical ace, was in the seconds immediately after a target emerged from FTL—

'Ten and twelve.'

—when you couldn't tell if there was some unfortunate sod right behind them, following them down the same pipe.

'Ah balls,' Lex chirped. 'Three new returns.'

'The target?'

'Hightailing.'

SixJen might've felt smug about the whole thing – *tolja* – if she'd had room in the remnants of her emotional brain for anything but a ghostly flicker of anger.

On screen the *Shattergeist* dropped like a stone – that same perpendicular dodge it'd used against the rival merc last time she'd had it in sight. But the missiles didn't even twitch in their course.

Fizzing innocently in the fugitives' place, still wreathed in all the diminishing wyrdlight of the FTL spout they'd spiralled down, like fresh-faced kiddies who'd chased a puppy into a fucking firing range, three manifestly undefended media ships popped into corporeality and replaced the 'Geist's heat signature.

'Taa-daaa,' Lex mumbled mournfully.

They were swallowed in fire.

SixJen thought perhaps she might have seen one of them, the one spared a direct hit, limp onwards through the annihilation zone without being entirely atomised, but in the next second the chaos of combat unfurled all around her and the wellbeing of the journalists dropped from the list of her priorities.

The *Shattergeist* let rip towards the cops. Arcing way off to the side, max-geeing inwards across the sunrise on the planet's terminator, spitting ordnance.

The runner's not supposed to scheme!

'It's a bait run,' SixJen barked. 'Weak ordnance! Don't buy it. She's got bigger explodo than that in there. Just wants to draw you into a dogf—'

The cops ignored her a second time. *Yee-haw*ing off to engagement and, in all likelihood, molecular death. SixJen didn't even bother to sigh, so entirely was she unsurprised.

'Boss?' Lex said, fireblooms tracking across the scanner. 'What action?'

We know this game. You watch, hunter. You watch the fight—

The cops circling. Doing a little better than she'd feared, at least. Like binary suns, keeping the prey between and in front, caught in their crossfire—

You watch the fight and when the prey's exhausted, ohhh … when she's weak and ready to die. Then—

'You gonna dial back?' Lex supposed. Only a hint of boredom in the tinny voice. 'Play possum, right? Watch 'til the critical moment.'

Then you strike.

Except.

Except the woman in the *Shattergeist* had seen through all of it last time. Knew the game. Knew it well enough to plan three moves ahead.

Except the fugitive ship wasn't playing the way the cops wanted today either. Their vicious little ménage-á-trois – like remoras orbiting a shark – spoilt again and again by the fugitives coughing out unexpected gouts of plasma from hidden pods, or somersaulting without warning to pursue a new course, or casually slicing off *this* cop's autogun, *that* cop's chaff-bay.

The runner, SixJen figured, had been running too long not to've learnt a thing or two about the hunt.

She wants to be caught.

But she won't let herself stop.

'No possum today,' SixJen said, grabbing the liminals and pressing forwards.

The Viper surged ahead with a tremble – sluggish and stupid feeling after SixJen's years dancing in the *The*, but a target was a target was a target.

'And me?' Lex sounded giddy. 'You want me t—'

'You stay where you are.' She worked her jaw, reminding herself how to fly a crapheap. 'Need you to plan me a oneshot. Pinpoint, Lex. Take out an engine. Nothing flashy, nothing traceable.'

'I can … yeah, I can do that … It won't get through that bloody thing's shields, mind …'

'You're not aiming at the fugitive.'

'What?'

The battle thundered in silence.

This close the temptation was almost unbearable. This close the numbness seemed to crack; the excitement – the anticipation – bubbling through. This close to the prey SixJen almost believed she could *feel* things again.

Looping. Hammering out the lead. Letting targeting solutions construct and dissolve. Making a show of it.

The runner.

Fuck, she's right there.

'Got that vector for you,' Lex mumbled for the third time.

'Stand by. And shut up.'

Yeah, this close up—

(—as the *Shattergeist* passed and dived and spiralled, as its cornerless shadow shifted across the plastic curve of Shibboleth below/above/beside, as she and the cops jinked and tumbled through and around the yacht's fields of fire—)

—this close, the urge to really let rip, to load the batteries and heave every deathbringer the Viper could muster, to vomit, to self-invert, to turn its own pods inside out in one great guttural orgasm of weaponry, to incinerate the *Shattergeist* in a single galaxy-rupturing clap of nuclear Armageddon, to *finish this now*, was almost too much to bear.

Adrenaline, Jen. Poetic excitement. You remember this?

Only the voice deep inside. Only the coldness, only the numbness. Only that stopped her.

Look at the shields on that thing. (The cops' rounds disintegrating into walls of iridescence, barely troubling the armour beneath.)

They've upgraded and upgraded, the little bastards. (Her own shots caroming and dissolving; magazines depleting with horrific speed.)

They're richer than senators and tougher than a cruiser.

You can't win this the stupid way, huntress.

Be smart.

79

Be smart not strong.

And so she held her place in the spinning flock: an intricate executive-toy orrery of insane concentricities and plutonium-tipped lines. Playing her part.

One of the cops, demonstrating significantly less restraint, let slip a salvo containing essentially everything remaining in his magazine. Whooping as he did so. To his credit the fusillade briefly overstretched the *Shattergeist*'s port-side shields, dumping them to death in an ionic haze for all of one second, and in that instant of weirdly infectious triumph (as both she and the other Viper instinctively focused fire), the fugitive ship was knocked spinning by the transmitted force.

And SixJen saw the chance coming.

'Get ready,' she hissed to Lex.

The *Shattergeist* righted itself with a conspicuous jerk, shields re-forming, and puked out a miniature vision of hell. Like: *anything you can do I can do better.* SixJen couldn't help imagining the crazy-haired she-creature within – *sad eyes, sad eyes!* – stabbing at random controls in fury while her ball-less boyfriend whimpered and whined.

The cop who'd dared to wing her took the brunt of it. *You pissed her off, pal.*

In fact the *Shattergeist*'s instinctive retaliation, if that's what it was, managed to be weirdly accurate despite the petulance SixJen was imagining. She and the other cop were treated to a firestorm which was merely withering, but the cavalier pilot who'd taken his big shot? He was all but crushed. His shields shredded like paper, his armour flensed in three places, and with a modicum of sense SixJen wouldn't have credited he ceased all whooping, turned the ragged remnants of his own coffin back towards Shibboleth, and ran like hell, spheres of smoke bubbling in his wake.

'*Now*,' SixJen said.

SixJen didn't see Lex's rail-shot coming. Nobody did: scanners still whited out by the barrage. She never saw it hit home either, though she was watching for both. But as the *Shattergeist* accelerated to chase the half-dead cop, as SixJen had known it would – *because that's the fun option, isn't it, you nutty little bitch?* – in that moment the *other* cop discovered his aft starboard engine had suddenly and mysteriously been annihilated.

'Uh,' he said over the radio. 'M-miss?' Beginning to lean hard right.

A ghastly little chain reaction rattled across the hindparts of his craft, all directionless sparks and zero-gee vapour. The other engine couldn't take the strain, the gas-thrusters couldn't fight the gravity well, and as he burbled and swore down the radio his craft tilted unmistakably towards the muddy pearl of Shibboleth.

'What is it?' she said. Not even bothering to aim for 'sympathetic'.

'Miss I … gotter tellyer. S-spokerther the Commander. Said keeper fugertive busy longas perssible. Got a … a consultant onroot, he sez. Sordit all out.'

SixJen scowled, a hoarfrost prickle in her spine. 'Consultant?'

'FIA, he sez.'

Federal Intelligence Agency.

Why the fuck would—

'You … You thinkyer can keeper fugertive busy foruz, miss? L-likehe sez? Cuz I think … I think I ent able mself.' His Viper was oozing away and down now, tumbling slowly, accreting a warm wash of exofriction. Doomed.

'I suggest you bail,' SixJen snapped down the line, terse, putting the word 'consultant' from her mind. *Not now*. Then

81

closed the link so she wouldn't have to listen to him rant and rave. Kneading the bridge of her nose.

FIA.

Shit.

She drummed her fingers against the liminals. Watched the little Viper descending into the exosphere on the scanner.

Made a decision.

With a quiet 'huh' she began stabbing at her consoles, plotting a specific course and appealing to the vessel's rudimentary intelligence to pursue a very particular end.

'Boss …' Lex interrupted, his voice as low (not very) as it could get.

'Not now.'

'Boss, if I didn't know better—'

'Quiet.'

'—I'd, uh. I'd say you were plotting an intercept course, there.'

She ignored him. Glanced at the scanner. Cop#1 was leading the *Shattergeist* on a doomed yet oh-so-merry chase across the planetary dawn, a hundred kliks away and more, trailing amputated spacejunk as they flew. Closer to home Cop#2 was fluking gently into an untroubled roll which, for all its graceful grandeur, was unmistakable to SixJen's eye as a death spiral. Beneath it lay nothing but a series of exponentially tightening curves towards the planet, a catastrophic encounter with its mesopause and an inglorious death being cheesegrated to nothingness by the atmosphere.

The pilot took her advice, ejecting in a spume of frozen gases and the swaddling plastifields of a RemLok, carried to a more sustainable orbit by its miniature thrusters.

Whereupon, like the magnificently predictable idiot he was, he fired up his OhShit-beacon without even waiting for the Bad Guy to exit stage left.

82

Which suited SixJen just fine.

'Bo-oss …'

'Lex.'

'Boss, it … it kind of looks from here like you just lowered your shields.'

'Lex, I'm going to need another firing solution.'

'But—'

'You'll know when.'

'A-and until then what's—'

'I'm just stepping outside.'

The cop was sweating in his suit. Steaming his faceplate. His hyperventilations down the radio made her feel like he was breathing in her ear.

'Repeat after me,' she said. '*You shouldn't have left us alive up here.*'

'Yer … yer sherdnta left us 'live upere.'

They floated together, otherwise profoundly alone, above the great pregnant bulge of Shibboleth.

'*We'll hunt you down …*'

'W … wull untyer down…'

'*You dismal syphilitic slut-coward …*'

'You … you dismal s … siff …'

'*Syphilitic.*'

'Syph …litik …'

'Good. *Slut-coward …*'

'Slut-cowerd …'

'*And dedicate our lives to taking revenge upon you.*'

'A-and dedercate urlives ter … ter takin' revenge onyer.'

'Now close the commline.'

The cop, currently drifting upside down relative to her, thumbed a control on the sleeve of his RemLok. SixJen activated her own OhShit-beacon.

Come get us, bitch.

'Well done,' she told him. 'I didn't think one target would work, you see.'

'I ... I dunno whatyer mea—'

'Now please be quiet.' She flicked channels on the cuff of her own suit, obliterating him and his noisy breath from her attention. 'Lex?'

'Here.'

'Sitrep.'

'It's ... it's been a bit bloody frantic out there, boss.'

It had been years since SixJen had ejected from a ship. She'd forgotten how cloying the RemLok suits could be, the smell of plastic and ozone, how dangling adrift in the emptiness could engender a contradictory mix of agoraphobia and claustrophobia. How the instinct to cluster together with anyone else likewise drifting, to seek out solidity and matter purely to define one's place against a canvas that defied all perspective, could override all other concerns.

No wonder those cargo men from the news reports had herded themselves into such convenient swarms. It was all she could do not to reach out and grip the hand of the cop. He'd already groped for similar contact once or twice himself.

She'd brushed him away, of course.

'Go on,' she told Lex, dismissing everything else from mind. Sometimes the numbness was a virtue.

'Okay, so ... first we had our friendly psychopathic damage-junkies – this is about three hundred kliks from your position – we had 'em right on the verge of wiping out Idiot Cop#1, in his oh-so-thoroughly-already-fucked-up boat. Wheeeen all of a sudden another Viper – the one *you* were told not to damage, if I'm not mistaken, but recently ejected from anyway – comes pelting along at stupid speed to kamikaze right into their shields.'

84

'Any damage?'

'Bit. Nothing worth talking about. I told you – those kids are *fortified*.'

Dammit.

'Then?'

'Well … They're pissed off, right? Finished off Cop#1 in a jiffy. Maybe went a bit over the top with that.'

'I saw the flare. Killkure?'

'Killkure.'

'And?'

'And then … well. They're right on the verge of buggering off, aren't they, when – wouldn't you know it – this weird message comes over the radio. Seems Cop#2 is out of his raft and enjoying a little vacswim. Wanted to send our fugitive pals a friendly declaration of a vendetta. I believe the words "syphilitic slut-coward" came up. You happen to know anything about that, boss?'

'Did the *Shattergeist* get the message?'

'Oh, I think so.'

'Why?'

''Cos they turned right round, boss. And 'cos they're now heading your way at, ah … at *some speed*.'

SixJen nodded to herself. Peered past her own feet. Clawed back the waves of dizzying panic at the distance below, the storms chasing across the planetary camber, the paparazzi flash-flares of lightning from above. That thought, in its turn, sent her eyes scanning nearspace. Sure enough, lurking like a vulture before a kill, the last remaining media ship, scarred and dented in the crucible of its arrival, had taken up position a few dozen kliks from their spot. These two twitching, tiny, tantalising targets.

Great TV.

The frightened cop reappeared on her radio. 'M-miss?'

She glanced sideways at him, barely able to see his face through the condensed sweat. 'M-miss? Miss, thersa *voice* onner line! I-it, it—'

'What did she say?'

'It … she … she sez "heads up". A-and then larfter lot.'

'Huh.' She flicked lines again. 'Lex.'

'They're travelling, boss.'

'ETA?'

'Fifteen.' *Shit. So fast!*

'You know what to do?'

'I … I think so, b—'

'Lex, what're they doing with their shields?'

'That's the … Boss, they're … They're still up.'

No. No, that's not what …

What about your fun, bitch?

You turn them off you turn them off you turn them off—

SixJen thought … like a dream … she thought she could see them. A pinprick of light, growing. No sense of scale or speed. Just a stealthy star, a tunnel, a *javelin* of flame.

Incoming.

'Seven seconds. No change.'

Shit shit shit.

'Fire.'

'What?'

'You heard me!' *Five. Four.* 'Fire, Lex! She'll drop them.' *She'll drop the shields. She's got to.* 'You fire right past us.'

The light.

Three.

The ionic glint of shields. The *Shattergeist* coming to smear them across the stars.

Two.

'But I could h—'

'Just do it!'

86

Seven

Myq worked it out on the way down. Moments of eerie clarity packaged neatly between uncharacteristic outbursts of anger at all of Tee's crazies (as if impending death had finally lubricated his brain and freed it from hormonal enslavement), and even more numerous stints of spiralling, shrieking panic.

We're going to die!

Plus sensory interruptions of a more sexual nature. Tee was getting frisky while they dropped from the sky. Of course.

The eerie clarity part:

'The merc!' he snarled. 'The fucking merc ship was hiding in the atmosphere! It was there all along!'

It was the only plausible explanation. The sneaky shit had been sniping at the battle from below, shielded from their scanners, hidden amidst the stratospheric clouds which the *Shattergeist* was, even now, bumbling and rolling its way through, venting fuel. Myq recalled a moment, mid-battle, while Teesa was occupied with squealing and blasting at the first Viper, in which one of its lagging comrades had abruptly limped into an orbital plunge on the scanner. Had that been due to the merc too? A missed shot? A test run? Or – *oh crap* – baiting the path?

Setting Tee up for that last, headlong, murderous strike?

… which implied – *crap crap crap* – that someone else considered his girlfriend's frighteningly psychotic desire to mulch spacewalkers an entirely predictable piece of behaviour.

All of which musings had led, inevitably, to the Uncharacteristic Anger part of his oscillating mood:

'You … you dropped our shields, Tee. *Again!*' Flapping his finger at her. 'W … why did you have to drop our shields?'

She gurgled something indecipherable. Possibly '*it's more fun that way.*' Her mouth was full.

Myq wasn't going to let her calm him down this time, not in the midst of a full-blown and frankly rather enjoyable tantrum. 'Why do you do *anything?*' he snarled. *I am soooo bored of being the boring one.* 'We're going to fucking *die!*'

They probably weren't, of course. They'd spent literally gajillions – Teesa assured him that was a real number – upgrading the ship and its systems, wanky music software and all, precisely so they wouldn't have to do too much thinking/worrying/giving-a-shit about the fiddly stuff in between all the Blowing Things Up.

Still, with a medium-sized rocky planet rising to meet you at some considerable speed it felt rather good to flap and shout.

It had all happened so fast anyway. They'd almost been upon the spacesuited cops when the hammer fell. A pair of thrashing bodies expanding hugely on screen, Tee's excitement almost indecent in all its babbling, shivering absorption. (And worse, in all its infectiousness. Myq hadn't exactly rushed to stop her, had he?)

She'd unshielded the *Shattergeist* a scant half-second before impact, purring to herself. But in that same instant (*how did the merc know?*) the thunderbolt hit. A mag-projectile, he supposed, launched with exquisite care from directly behind the targets, streaking venomously between them, down amidst

88

the umbral mass of planetary thunderheads. He felt abstractly (impossibly) as though he'd caught a glimpse of it – some unreal blur; a streak of the reaper's scythe – before it struck.

Certainly its grim results had been perceptibly instant: one moment they'd been making a beeline for the cops, the next they were spinning, several hundred metres distant, sirens shrieking and main engines obliterated.

Why didn't the merc kill us? he wondered – a seedy little thought amidst the morass. *He – or she – could've skewered us like a bloody whale.*

Why knock us down instead of wiping us out?

But.

But.

But.

Falling, falling, falling. No time, no brainspace, no sensory energy. Not as he moved seamlessly back to the Panic portion of his mental cycle and hammered impotently against the controls. Not with lights whirling and klaxons klaxoning and Teesa – unapologetic, uncowed, gurgling and delighted by the whole thing – doing something insane in his lap.

'Frhop bnn shlli,' she said. *Stop being silly.* Probably. 'Whuh*nt* gnna duh.'

'We are! We *are* going to die! We're—'

Quite abruptly the alarms died. The clouds thinned around them to a scrawny strata of turbulent steppes and peaceful plateaus, and Myq caught his first crazed glimpses of the surface far beneath. Green. Misted. Dank.

The computer cycled through re-entry solutions, stabilisers hissing. And little by little the *Shattergeist* restored a modicum of balance.

Myq felt weirdly robbed, still shuddering with pent-up emotion.

[AUTO TOUCHDOWN.] the status-holo said, picked out in a reassuring shade of green. **[REPAIRS REQUIRED. SEEKING LANDING ZONE.]**

[PLEASE DO NOT INTERFERE WITH THE AUTOPILOT PROTOCOLS.]

[PLEASE RELAX AND ENJOY THE DESCENT.]

The bloody thing even started playing soothing music without being asked.

'Thank NoGod for that,' he murmured.

Which is when Teesa reached up blindly from his crotchal regions and gave the stick – the *control* stick – a violent yank.

'What are you *doing* what are you *doing* what are you d—'

The alarms started again. The ship banked furiously into another deadzone of hi-alt vapours, rattling and roaring at each cloudstrike, flipping end over end. Gravity starting to uncomfortably declare its presence.

Myq tried not to puke. Tried not to come. Tried not to cry.

Laughed a bit.

Teesa just giggled and bent back to her task.

'The merc was in the atmosphere,' she said, a miniature maybefrown troubling her brow. 'Just like you said.' Rain, not *proper* rain, not *back home* rain; just an insipid layer of hanging damp, like fog with added gravity, fizzed round her shoulders.

'S-so?' Myq was still shaking.

'Soooo, chances are they were still watching us on the way down. They could've killed us up there if they'd wanted, yes? But they chose not to. Why?'

'I … I don't …'

She flicked rainwater off a vast overhanging … thing. Probably a leaf. It made a noise like a startled mouse and curled up, turning orange. She grinned hugely.

'Look, if we'd come down in a niiiiice long straight line – smash, re-entry, *swooooosh* – they would've known exactly where to look. And then we could've found out what they had in mind. Would you have preferred that, Myq?'

He sulked. 'No.'

'Well then. Little bit of random course adjustment never hurt anyone.' She flapped a hand around herself – the ship, the rain, the mud, the *jungle* – and grinned. 'Isn't this *supernebular*?'

She'd touched them down, refusing to let the autopilot handle things personally, just as the *Shattergeist*'s fuel reserves were honking and spuffling in alarm. Part gliding, part landing, part flying on fumes. What she called a 'little bit of random course adjustment' was, more accurately, the most terrifying stratotumble imaginable: crazily shifting course every few seconds, ploughing through cloudbanks, dodging gaseous spore-bird-flopping-whale-whatnots, always lashed by rain, always chased by lightning, always shouting and protesting and shrieking like a child.

At least, *he* was. She just kept blowing him. Glancing up to tweak the liminals now and then like she knew where she was going. Like (*oh NoGod*) like she'd planned the whole damn thing.

And yes, thank you, obviously: he'd obediently orgasmed at the point of touchdown. Skull-breaking terror or not. *Pathetic.*

She pointed out into the jungle like she owned the place. 'That outpost's not far, sweetie. Looked pretty big on the scans. Couple of miles? We'll get repairs there, don't you fret.'

She knew it was there before we even started to drop.

'Hang on, we can't just—'

'Walk in the woods! Walk in the woods!' She disappeared into the tangle of (*don't look too close*) undergrowth, humming to herself.

The worst part, Myq decided, gawping in the silence, the most revolting headache-inducing part of it all, worse than the sweaty pressure of endoclimatisation – the gravity aches, they called it – and the sticky wraparound alien sense-bombardment, worse than the annoying hoot-squawks of distant wildlife and the twitchy responses of the hair-triggered local plants, was this:

She was right.

All that smashing and bashing around on the way down. All that chaos. All that crazed giggling inanity.

Eminently bloody sensible.

Avoiding pursuit.

So why couldn't she just have told him what she was up to? Why wait until the end? Why couldn't she trust him enough to … to own up to her scheme?

C'mon, Myquel. He dragged a hand across his upper lip, dangerously close to a schoolboy blub. *This isn't about the crash landing and you know it.*

And, ohhh, it wasn't. There was a bigger picture here. A macro to the micro – every bit as infuriating. A sneaking suspicion that had been settling over him for days, that down in the fuzzy abyss of Teesa's rampage, down in the murky depths of her mercurial, spontaneous, vicious, unpredictable, *beautiful* self … there was a method behind the madness.

The inkling had arisen drop by drop. The way she'd spoken to that reporter, back on Tun's Wart. The way her voice changed sometimes, airbursting with innocuous-seeming wisdom (*the lifecycles of fucking shibboletti, for NoGod'ssake*). The things she mumbled in her sleep. The refusal to speak of the past. The way he caught her staring sometimes, out into the dark, lips moving, eyes wet.

Something.

Going.

On.

The kicker? The kicker had come just a few moments before, as they'd stepped from the *Shattergeist* and tramped out into the mud, stumbling through puddles of rainwater already gathering in the blast craters round its jets. He'd caught her just then, pausing at the ship's consoles under the auspices of locking it down, dialling into Shibboleth's rudimentary info-net.

Checking the prices of shibboletti glands. Smiling softly to herself.

And the crazy part? He wouldn't have minded if she just owned to it. If she'd just volunteered the information. It wasn't like he was going to quit on her. Come what may, come what shenanigans, come what secret motives, he would've gone along with Teesa anyway: *good little puppydog, good little slave.* They both knew it.

(*Weak! weak!*)

So why couldn't she just explain it all? Why not confess there was some … plan unfolding? Some design beneath the destruction? Something to do with those idiot fart-creatures … their priceless glands … and maybe (*surely!*) the man who'd once owned Teesa as a slave?

'*A commodity baron, let's say,*' the dead reporter had said. Sneering and sweating below his camera-eye. '*All above board. Someone in … ohhh … someone in the glander-trade.*'

Why? Why wouldn't she tell him?

And worse: why couldn't Myq just fucking *ask* about it?

Standing in the clearing with the ship steaming and clicking behind him, rain soaking into his clothes, he made a decision:

I'm not going to follow her.

Not until she comes back. Not until she comes back and … and we set off together. Side-by-side. No more puppydog.

93

He crossed his arms. Set his jaw. Sniffed.

Then Teesa made a sound, already far further into the foliage than he would have guessed, like something between a laugh and a scream, and he was sprinting through creepy trees and sulphur-puffing creepers before he even realised it.

Weak! Weak! Weak!

He found her crooning in a gallery of looming palms, bent over a clutch of wriggling worm-things nesting amidst sticky fronds of viscous jelly in the trough of a stump. The anonymous microfiends (to Myq's eyes and nostrils the most fitting descriptor would be 'turds with teeth') kept puffing themselves up, turning purple and orange, and strutting across their miniature stage as if for Teesa's approval.

But they, alas, were not the principal catchers of Myq's eye as he stumbled to a halt.

'Oh Myquel,' Teesa trilled, not looking round. 'They startled me when I went by, but – look! Aren't they wonderful?' She poked one hard enough to break it in half. It didn't seem to mind.

Around her the forest itself was changing. Fingerlike fronds of great tarantula-plants uncoiling towards her, chromatic pattern-displays flushing and chasing along their stems. Small creatures, apparently drunk, kept dropping from the canopy to wriggle and mewl, farting little puffs of rank powder and flashing bright tones. Something vaguely birdlike alighted on a branch and started strutting for all it was worth, puffing out little iridescent pockets of mazelike blood vessels, squawking like a fucking moonjuice-junkie at the end of a bad trip. Proudly showing off what Myq assumed was its genitals.

In a bubble all round Teesa, marked by clashing colours, trembling branches and unfortunate noises, the forest of Shibboleth was slowly, obscenely, getting horny.

Like the reporters. Like the cops in the jail.
Like me, dammit.

Still. Even that wasn't what had arrested Myq's progress through the woods. He gave a small squeak and tried to breathe. Finger uncurling to point vaguely upwards.

'T-Tee …'

'Shibbo-shibbo-shibboletti,' she babbled happily. 'You can really tell those stupid bastards come from here, can't you? *All* these things … same weirdo space-monster genepool.' She flicked one of the worm-creatures hard enough to make it pop. 'Fat, farty, spore-spouting little gasbags.' He'd never seen her happier.

'Teesa. Teesa, stay still …'

'Y'know what? I bet that cloud layer we came through? I bet that's just, just spores. All of it. Hanging round up there. Imagine that, Myq. A whole planet wreathed in spunk.'

'Don't … move.'

She finally deigned to glance his way, perfect nose crinkling. Then slowly, unavoidably, tilted her head back to follow his finger.

It was a predator, he supposed. Toothy, tentacley, yadda yadda. Vaguely catlike, for the sake of argument, although only in as much as it was clinging halfway down a tree, back arched, ears (or, hell, leaves?) flattened against its boxlike head, with multiple rows of slitlike eyes fixed on Teesa's crown.

Growling.

'Naughty kitty,' she whispered.

There the familiarities ended. On its midriff a set of petal-like envelopes – rank, canvas-esque material – shuddered open to expose shocking blazes of wet purple and blue. Its teeth clearly weren't as solid as they appeared, shifting unpleasantly in its jaw, and where any self-respecting feline-analogue might have sported a muscular set of rear legs, *this* biologically-confused fucker exhibited what could only be described as a mighty pair of amorphous testicles, each half distended in a membranous flap holding it against the tree. It reminded Myq of nothing so much as a gigantic scrotal version of a chameleon's foot – which was apt, given that the saggy thing kept changing colour.

Teesa stood up, not remotely frightened. And dug, with a half-arsed urgency, for her little lasergun.

Which wasn't there.

The creature pounced.

In all the shrieking and terror that followed, as the surrounding wildlife variously honked and coiled and – in one or two overexcited cases – exploded in fungal puffs, as Myq saw Teesa for the first time *truly* frightened, *truly* desperate, *truly* uncool, the unlovely thought uncoiled in his mind that it was anybody's guess whether the fiend was trying to eat her or mate with her.

The creature's lithe body slammed onto her, forelimbs pushing then pinning her even as the ballbag-suckerpad engulfed her shins. She cried out, trying to get away, hammering at its head with her fists, scattering leaf litter and bright mushrooms. Acid-trip tendrils whipped from the beastie's eyes (that is, what Myq'd *thought* were eyes) to restrain her hands and hold steady her head. And something … something very, very, slimy … lollopped from its jaw like a great internal prolapse and began, unmistakeably, to stiffen.

'Big boy, huh?' Teesa whispered, as if in a dream. Eyes like moons.

And Myq? Myq, whose feet hadn't moved in a minute. Myq, whose body had turned to glass. Myq, who was abstractly aware of an irritating trickle of sweat down the cleft of his arse—

Myq discovered he hadn't felt quite so important in weeks.

He giggled.

Pulled out the laser he'd stolen from Tee's clothes several days earlier – a safety measure, he'd told himself – and shot the monster through the head.

Under his breath, hoping she didn't hear, he whispered:

'*She's mine.*'

They fucked on the forest floor, right next to the puddle of monstergunk. Tee kept pausing to shoot at the smaller animals and plants which came slithering by, unable to resist her magnetic pull. Myq understood then, under the fog, under the sighs and smiles, that he already knew – that perhaps he'd *always* known – why Teesa didn't share her plans. And why he'd never dare ask.

Planning? Motives? Agendas? Such things were the hallmarks of the Merely Ordinary. Myq needed to believe Tee was above all that. He needed from her the illusion of perfect and spontaneous *performance*. He needed her to excuse and validate his own dingy narcissism; to make him feel like a force of nature rather than just another clammy notoriety-junkie.

Above all? He needed to believe she didn't care about anything but him and the thrill. Anything else – any tawdry Plan – was simply Competition for her attention.

... oooor *some* sort of overly-wanky, self-distractionary skyshit like that. Frankly, two days later, bombed off his tits on local glandnarcs, Myq's predilection for pompous inner analysis was raging hard.

The pair had bumbled out of the forest into the damp outskirts of the farmtown, Gridsyne, clumsily disguised by smart-fabric hats and hoods, in the middle of a convenient storm which had all but cleared the streets. They'd spent the majority of the first two solar days shacked up in a cheap guesthouse, dyeing their hair and remote-ordering new clothes, studiously working their way through the veritable cornucopia of drugs – door-delivered – derived from Shibboleth's balloonlike wildlife.

Hence existentially lubricated, Myq's new theory about his own wilful ignorance went some way, at least, to explain why he hadn't stirred himself, nor become too dramatically annoyed, when Tee leaned out of bed during the first night to make a series of scrambled arrangements down the phone with a local shibboletti-trade agent.

'Five hundred head of livestock,' she'd snapped, winking at Myq as if daring him to ask.

I bloody won't.

'Yes,' she'd said, blowing him a kiss. 'Yes, all podded, good to go.'

She looks stupid with black hair, he told himself, stroppy.

Which she didn't. She looked amazing.

'Well, *obviously* I'll be wanting them delivered. No – not far. Big clearing, couple of miles west of town. Talk to … wait, hang on – Myq? What was the chopshop called?'

'Grundle's.'

'Talk to someone down at Grundle's repair yard on the main strasse, would you? They're running some repairs on-site. They'll have coordinates. Mm-hmm. Mm-hmm. Oh, I expect they've already run a freight path through the jungle. They're quite, ah, *extensive* repairs.'

Extensive = expensive, Myq gloomily daydreamed. Their one and only excursion into the crackling cultural cauldron that was Gridsyne had involved a sheepish conference with a suspicious ultrafatty at a machine shop in town. The man'd almost fallen out of his gut-barrow for laughing when Myq, sporting freshly ginger hair and a blend-in-with-the-locals beige kilt, presented the job.

Saud Kruger gold-class Dolphin, complete replacement thruster-module and general repairs.

'And a new paint job,' Tee had chimed in. 'Something in pink.'

It was only when Myq started naming numbers – astronomical, stupid, impossible numbers – then infotabbed through a Proof Of Funds order from their still relentlessly-swelling account, that the man had started to take them seriously. And even then, probably, only because Tee's weird influence had stolen over him.

'Righ',' he'd said, blushing, signing a work-order. 'G-giz furdays.'

Four days had quickly turned into two. Plus, *ahem*, not a word spoken to anyone, *you understand*, at the fair fair price of an extra zero on the end of the quote. It was roughly the same arrangement Tee lazily made, hours later – *don't ask, Myq, don't ask, don't ask* – in negotiations with the live-stock guy.

Five hundred shibboletti, he thought, *delivered right to the ship. Secret as you like.*

No questions asked, no answers given.

More expensive than a platinum planet.

It was nice being rich.

'Uh, Tee—?'

'Mm?'

Don't fucking ask, idiot!

'Nothing.'

It was nice being rich and weak.

So they smoked and they fucked and they lazed about in a room so gobsmackingly boring that all of Myq's neurotically-programmed zen – *don't ask! don't ask!* – was strained to breaking point. They screwed and they snorted and they listened to the rain, and they whiled away hours on the local sensenet learning the rich (ugh) and varied (ugh) history of Shibboleth and its (ugh) culture. And then all at once, just as it darkened on the second evening, Tee quite abruptly threw a wobbler.

'I want,' she hissed. 'To *dance*.'

Fuzzy brained, stoned, it took Myq a moment or two to dislodge himself from engrossment in what passed for news on Shibboleth's net – *stock prices peaking!; septuagenarian eaten by lumbartree!; unscheduled official arrives from Federation!;* plus a dozen gossipy articles on the *Shattergeist* and its occupants – and looked round just in time to be struck in the face by a ballistic pillow.

'We,' Teesa declared, stamping a foot, 'are going *out*.'

Myq thought about arguing. Even flopped his mouth open and shut a few times, venting an exciting waveform of purple smoke (which itself occupied his attention for thirty seconds longer than it should have). Ultimately he decided, in a powerful cascade of logic and experience, that however sensible his arguments Teesa could be relied upon not to listen.

'Fine,' he grunted, glancing back at the netscreen. His own face stared back, harassed-looking above a senseform tag marked WANTED in a dozen languages. 'But we'll need to keep a low profile.'

Somewhere not far off, Teesa was already clomping down the guesthouse stairs.

Eight

Sonic schizophrenia.

Acoustic Armageddon.

A great crushing cataract of obscene noise wrapped round her, drowned her. Weaponised vocals inducing a wince with every line. A beat so close to subaudible it entered the realms of the metaphysical, shooting tremors not only into SixJen's bones, teeth and eyes but resonating weirdly – or so she abstracted – in the vicinity of her spirit.

The FerkinLowhd Nightclub, Gridsyne city. Wet, dark, strobe-lit, evil.

The clientele: farmkids in toxic makeup, come from their homesteads for a long weekend. Swaggering townboys with hormonal groinlights flickering green or red. Drunk idiots leering and laughing, androgyny dialled high, bodies hot and sweaty and stinking; goonish accents rendered even less decipherable by volume. And the whole unseemly maggoty mass twitching, throbbing and jerking with mindless regularity – whether ostensibly dancing or otherwise – to the invasive leprous beat.

Like a great hand, SixJen thought, yanking every puppet string all at once.

She moved through the crowd and Hated.

It was odd, she reflected, eyes sweeping left-right-left, finger tracing the single rivet on her gun butt, how the impending end of her thirteen-year hunt could dredge up whatever meagre leavings of emotion remained inside her. It'd happened before, of course. In the battle with the Cobra, weeks earlier. In those dizzying instants, just two days ago, when the *Shattergeist* came to pulverise her and the idiot cop as they dangled in orbit. And now. It was happening now.

Like a taster. Like a perverse preview of the Holy Reward, except rich with irritation instead of the joy it supposedly granted.

And, yes, like a promise.

The runner: *near.*

But every time …? Every time, so far, the little witch had managed to get away. Every time the buzz died. The numbness trickled back – part soothing, part abominable. *Not now. Not this time.*

The truth was, there was simply nowhere else the fugitives could be. Lex had lost the sneaky little shits below the sporeclouds whilst dutifully rescuing SixJen and the drifting cop. The little computer had obediently traced the last-known trajectory of the *Shattergeist* to its logical end and found only unblemished forest. On a planet of almost endless jungle, studded only by farming frontiers and midsized glander-towns like Gridsyne, it was anyone's guess where they'd ditched.

A part of her, a tiny, ugly part, wished she'd instructed Lex to destroy them rather than simply knocking them down. *Finish it. Make it stop.*

But no, that's not how the hunt worked. The killing blow had to be by the hunter's hand. No minions, no help, no complications, no exceptions.

My kill.

Nobody else's.

My kill to make. My word to whisper.

'Boss?' Lex now said, back in his accustomed place on her lapel, coning-down his voice with a clever wave-transform so she – and only she – could hear him. 'We've got c—'

'I know. Shhh.'

Aberrant particles: on the edge of her senses and the edge of the crowd. Little motes of Wrong; the subtle distortions in an otherwise innocent scene which betrayed the perfect camouflage of a predator. Like the sound of someone trying to be quiet. Like still grasses on a windy day.

Cops.

They were twitching along with the music, at least. That showed willing. Spread out, slumped, out of uniform. But in all their preoccupied oversight, all their surveillance-op concentration, still it wasn't quite right: infinitesimally off-rhythm. They were trying too hard. Trying, SixJen grimly supposed, to impress. Alas, in a room packed with drugged-up noddies, each so lost in astrochemical communion that their own responses to the music had become involuntary, unconscious, as biological an imperative as a beating heart or a blinking eye; in the midst of all *that* Shibboleth's best Undercover Operatives stuck out like the proverbial Damaged Digit.

She wondered idly if they'd clocked her too. Decided it didn't matter.

No more caution. No more fucking about. No more circling.

There are other sharks in this water.

Find the prey. Take the shot.

She'd delivered the cop to the central precinct two continents away just hours after the battle. He'd played his role – that of the shrieking baitworm – with convincing aplomb,

103

and whilst SixJen felt no particular obligation to reward his performance, Lex had patiently opined that making an enemy of the local cops, on top of everything else, was not a smart move. Even so, she hadn't intended to hang about at the LawCom HQ any longer than necessary: the fugitives' trail wouldn't stay warm for long and she had no intention of enduring the Commander's predictable fumings at the loss of his ships. And yet, to her surprise, the medal-bedecked moron barely registered her arrival, too occupied with flapping and panicking like a houseproud hostess on the eve of a party.

'He's onhim way,' he kept mumbling, dabbing at sweat and shooing about his staff. 'Scour thfurkin surface, youselot! Finder fugertives! We 'elp this bigdick onhim way, thurza big fat Fed'ration subsidy in it!'

'FIA,' the cop she'd rescued whispered conspiratorially. 'Consultant frumma Fed'ration. Toljer.'

For all its vaunted independence, all its pseudo-legal exports and cultivated cultural alienation, it seemed Shibboleth's administrators weren't quite stupid enough to reject the probings of the Federation's money-packed tendrils; even one as insidious as the Federal Intelligence Agency.

A spook.

A spook, coming here.

For my *fucking target.*

Maybe? Maybe it was a legit response to all the trouble Teesa and Myq had caused; all the unstoppable momentum of their media offensive; the perverse cultural black mirror their celebrity held up to the Federation's teeming masses. Maybe two idiot kids on a bubblegum rampage really did warrant the agency's clandestine attention. But probably not.

104

She'd caught herself running a nervous hand up and down the puckered meat of her left arm – *seven … seven and counting* – and had vacated the Police HQ in haste.

Find her.

Find her fast.

It hadn't been hard in the end – just frustrating. A simple matter of extrapolation. The *Shattergeist*'s fuel reserves at the moment it went down + the proximity of repair yards + the availability of viable landing sites and the likelihood (according to the insinuations of the on-net local guidebooks) of any given town's population honouring the terms of a chunky 'say nothing' bribe. Dodgy types, it transpired, were not in short supply on Shibboleth.

Lex had maintained a chirpy (i.e. aggravating) running commentary while crunching the numbers. Narrowing the field to six possible cities in the time it took him to simply say so. SixJen had calmly self-harmed throughout.

No unauthorised landings logged on the worldnet. No record of top-tier aerospace contracts being awarded. No rumours, no arched brows, none of the blooms of violence nor mass promiscuity she would've expected. In fact, the more conspicuously the fugitives had disappeared, the more Lex leaned towards his preferred destination.

Gridsyne. A town well-known as a slithering nest of secrets.

An arbitrary trawl through the settlement's recent trade records had coughed up a noteworthy order for thirty gallons of lurid pink paint, which SixJen took – with an unfamiliar flush of adrenaline – as confirmation of Lex's hunch. The *The*'s visual overflight of the town, revealing a freshly-gouged scar across the jungle, thick with freight-lugging megavehicles and repair rigs, simply settled the matter.

The *Shattergeist*, candyfloss-bright, wreathed in oxysparks and a more macho class of frontier robot, sat undergoing repair like a dirty secret in a forest clearing right outside town.

'You wanna set down here?' Lex'd asked.

She shook her head. 'They're not in there.'

'We could wait. Ambush.'

Other sharks. Other sharks …

'No. We find them. *Now.*'

That had been yesterday.

And now? And *now* and *now*–

Now a skinny drunkard, trendily stubbled on one cheek and rouged on the other, stumbled from the pulsating dance-floor mass and clapped hisher hand on SixJen's shoulder. 'Awigh' byooful?' heshe drawled.

SixJen calmly broke the youth's middle finger and, stepping swiftly into the throng, used the ensuing (albeit drug-delayed) howls to cover a damn good ogle round the club.

Kids. Kids and cops and cannonfodder.

Damp little Gridsyne could hardly be called a thrumming metropolis, they'd found. By the standards of the überstats and continental megabergs of the Federation or Empire it barely registered: a nothingtown of a mere fifty thousand or so souls. *Why here?* she kept wondering; intuiting by now that nothing the fugitive did was an accident. *Why did she come here?*

On the other hand, in context (that is, on a rainforest world without cultural network, bourgeois history, class-division or homegrown entertainment trade) Gridsyne was a Paradise to the grimy, frog-faced workers who called Shibboleth home. Constructed on and around a rocky mesa slowly being subsumed by the jungle, its overriding aesthetic was Big! Chrome! Cylinders! – a veritable pickle-shelf of megascale tincans and looping monorails. Every third structure appeared to hold either a hotel or hostel, testament to the town's draw on bored steaders from outlying ranches, and SixJen had despaired (theoretically speaking) of ever locating the fugitives. Ultimately the dual application of Money and Menaces down at the civic surveillance centre, followed by three hours of Lex sifting CCTV, had thrown up a single grainy image and a likely location.

(SixJen's heart, she recalled, had almost exploded as she stared at that picture. Loving couple, hand in hand, stealing furtively into a hostel. She somehow hadn't quite believed it until then. Hadn't let it sink in.

This world. Same ground. Same soil.

Here.)

The guesthouse was no good anyway, twisting the thumbscrews on her building anxiety. 'Ther've gonout,' the artfully-rude reception bot had announced. '*Darncin*', themzed.'

Again – the urge to lay an ambush. To wait, to be smart, to be sneaky. But SixJen was done waiting now. She was done waiting and the game had changed the instant the runner stopped running and SixJen could all but *feel* the other predator circling in the murk.

Thank goodness, then, that dreary little Gridsyne was home to just one skeevy late-night joint for the hordes of tedium-dodging kids to blow off steam.

Darncin', in this town, meant the FerkinLowhd Nightclub.

Packed to perishing point with slabfaced yokels, its clientele showed off all the trendy turns and modal moves they'd picked up from last season's Federation shows. Like a cargo cult to fashion, this lot: a fanfest to imported affectation. It was easy to spot the wronguns, here.

Cop. Cop. Cop.

At least three. And undoubtedly more in uniforms outside. And all of them, all those *hahaha* discreet bastards, in that broken moment when her honking finger-broken victim smashed glasses and overturned tables (milking hisher

107

dramatic pain a little too vigorously, to SixJen's eye), *all* of them turned to glance at a dark corner across the floor. As if checking Teacher was watching.

SixJen oozed to a natural halt. Heat and cold fighting across her skin. Fingertips questing – *gun, gun, gun.*

Was there someone there? Some shape lurking? Some trenchcoated goon; some sinister patch of darker-than-dark?

The.

Competition.

She was right not to have waited at the guesthouse. Right not to have waited at the *Shattergeist.* Still … impossible to tell who or what was brooding there. Not with the strobe lights deepening every darkness. Not with bodies squirming, tattoos illuminating left and right. Not with the beat distorting the air itself. Not with adrenaline, that half-remembered invader, that atom-splitter of the mind, choking her senses.

And not.

When *she*—

'Boss.'

—was right—

'Boss, look, isn't that–'

—*there.*

Time did what time does. The room went away. The gun.

Take it.

There.

The runner.

The runner and her slave. Slow dancing. Sealed inside themselves. Close and classy and kind – smiling eyes, smiling mouths – in a bubble, a swamp, a sex-stinking festerpit of kissing, touching, rubbing kids. All round them. Ignored.

The gun.

No waiting.

Sharks. Cops. Competition.

This wasn't the old game. No shields, no ships, no plasma bombs. This wasn't how SixJen worked. But at the end of the world, on the cusp of the Great Reward, as the golden bough snapped and the hunter roared and the runner recoiled—

She raised the gun.

'Boss—'

Breathed.

There.

The fugitives saw her.

People (on another planet, on another plane) started to scream.

There!

A half-glance. She could spare the time. Nothing if not cautious. A stolen stare at that dark corner. Wary of jackals gazumping her prize.

Empty. She could see from here. Crazylight playing across it. *No threat.*

SixJen the killer laughed out loud for the first time in thirteen years, raised the gun to the face of the beautiful prey she'd chased twice across the galaxy, prepared to Say The Word—

—and watched with dreamlike detachment as her own hand opened like a smashed plum. As smoke and soot spumed on a crest of fragmented fingers (*mine*). As a gristle-thick wad of blood and bone (*mine, mine*) slapped into her eyes.

She dropped. Didn't mean to but did. Somewhere far away the screams stopped for an instant, swatted clear by a thunderclap to muffle the world, then resumed louder than before. And yet more distant.

Strange.

Heat and pain and a faraway wetness. The sound of water. None of it bothered her much, except insofar as it suggested someone had mercifully switched off the music.

A thought swam up.

The runner! Where's the r—

She became aware of movement. The herd shuffling and bolting as one, tangling towards the exit, spronking and whooping, as eerily synchronised in panic as in rhythm. The door was closed. No way out.

She clasped her good hand – her *only* hand, hahaha, *that's not funny* – to the lumpen mess she'd somehow discovered beneath the other wrist.

How did that happen? Things seemed greyer than usual.

She cast about herself for … for *what was it?* There was something important she was supposed to do. Nearby a young couple clenched one another hard at the heart of a growing space. For some reason the sight of them sent SixJen scrabbling for her gun – *no, no, idiot, not that hand, look at the mess you've made* – but even as she struggled with *that* instinct she realised neither youth was staring at her.

'Dammit boss boss get out he's behind you he's—'

It was a funny little voice. Someone chattering right into her ear. Right into her head, even. That didn't seem normal, but at the very least the shrill tones seemed to know what they were talking about. She obediently twisted to see.

Ah.

Things came back to SixJen in a rush. Like continents shifting. Like icebergs slamming down. The music hadn't stopped at all.

Just the sight of him, she supposed. The numbness slid back to cover the trauma. The pain dwindled away.

'Federal Agent,' the man shouted, just loud enough to be heard. No emotion in the voice. This time the music really did stop.

He had dead eyes. He had dead eyes and that was almost all SixJen needed to know. The clothes, the hair, the face: all preternaturally average. The badge: probably genuine. It didn't matter.

He wasn't looking at her anyway. Gun up, smoke coiling. Dundering local cops, all twitches and sweat on either side. Squawking kids packed together at the far edge of the room, pushing and panting.

He stepped past her. Paused, inches away, not looking down. Like she was beneath notice: an insect; an error; a *nothing*. His hand sneaking gently to hitch up the cuff of his left sleeve.

Three.

Scars.

SixJen nodded, just once. Theory ratified. Fears confirmed.

And then he strode onwards. Cops hustling into his wake like leaves on a stream, rifles levelled, boots kicking out to keep her down. All on another world.

Through their legs she watched the man who'd beaten her place his pistol against the woman she'd come to kill and say:

'Down.'

Grandstanding.

She curled a lip. A sudden insane desire to shout, *Fool!*

Don't you know how important this is? Don't you know how many times she's slipped away?

Don't talk! Don't look away! Don't perform!

Pull the trigger, prick! Kill her! Kill her and be done with it!

It's what *she* would've done.

'Down,' the man said again, waggling the gun. SixJen wondered if he had a name.

111

The runner sank to her knees. Her pretty little boyfriend, trembling, ghost-skinned, glossy with terror, tried to mumble something. Tried to protest, to interject – all damp hands and gangle-knees. Then gave a strangled cry and simply folded away, muzzlestruck. Bleeding. A maybeblur of movement round the agent's arm.

He's quick.

As if sharing her awe the crowd moaned, a low registration of sympathy. And the runner—

The runner simply stared down the gun barrel and smiled.

'For crimes too numerous to mention,' the agent monotoned, 'but principally the wanton destruction of Federal and corporate properties, and murder in the first degree, you are hereby sentenced to death.'

Making it look good, SixJen thought, clamping down on the wreck of her hand. *Making it look good so he's got a way out afterwards.*

Smart.

She knew better. Knew the man didn't give a crap about the crime nor the sentence. Didn't care for the Federation nor the Agency he served.

Just a smart cover for the hunt. A way of plugging into the galaxy. An ear to the wall of human affairs, like Captain goddamn Delino and his goddamn pirates.

(Had she, SixJen wondered at last, approached the whole thing the wrong way? Should she have been more *involved?* Entered *this* organisation or *that* clan? Been more dependent on the people amongst whom she hunted?)

Made no difference now, she supposed.

The agent straightened his arm. The crowd drew its breath. The runner didn't stop smiling.

'You've got the wrong person.' It came out of SixJen like

112

an escaping spirit. Without thought. Without fully understanding what she was saying or planning.

But far, far louder than necessary. *Making sure the kids can
hear.*

The man's head half twisted. 'What?'

'Her. She's. She's not who you think.'

'Don't be ridiculous. We both know who she is.'

'So say it.'

He sighed. A fair approximation of exasperation: habitual
rather than impulsive.

'Why?'

'Can't execute someone if you're not sure it's them,' she
said. Making it up.

The cops, she was dimly aware, traded glances. Looked
at the agent.

'Fine,' he said, shrugging. 'She is Teesa #32A[M/
Tertius]. Indentured property of one Madrien Axcelsus.
Abscondee. Fugitive. Murderer.' He started to turn back.

Got you, you little shit.

'But isn't that … isn't that the woman from the *Shattergeist*
we've heard so much about?'

'As well you know.'

'The … the one who's been destroying all those ships?
On the news?'

He turned his head fully at last, to face her. Eyes slen-
dered down. She wondered in that moment if he was feeling
it too: the rush of forgotten emotion, the death of numbness. If so, if his expression was indeed a mirror on his
thoughts, then the wash of triumphant smuggery infecting
him must have been intoxicating.

'I don't *have* to kill you,' he said, quietly. 'You know
that. You'll die anyway, afterwards. No reward. No
nothing.

'But frankly I'd far rather you saw it coming. Knowing. Do you understand? Knowing I won. Knowing I beat you. That would be nice. I think. But? If you say one more word? Trying to – *what*? To delay me? To buy time? Then I will shoot you in the belly. And your hunt will end in agony as well as defeat.'

She nodded, once. Wanting to scream.

Don't look round don't look round don't look round.

The agent turned away. Back to the Fugitive.

(She: still smiling. Eyes not even flickering. *She knows. She can see them coming. Don't look don't move an inch*—)

'Now,' said the man. Smiling indecently. 'Where were we?'

The crowd hit him like a hammer.

Like a cloud, it swallowed him. Boiled around. Slurping the cops into its mass, great sweating lips smacking shut, hair and bodies and tattoos and sequins. No gunshots fired. Fists flying, bones breaking. The mob, the fanboys, the farm-fanatics. The disciples defending their messiah. SixJen saw a uniformed arm spin from the mass; ragged tatters spuming in its wake. Someone screamed, someone laughed.

The name. That's all it had taken in the end. *Teesa. Shattergeist.*

Poor, culture-starved little Shibboleth. So empty of experience its own news-cycles were clogged with the *Shattergeist's* adventures. They'd come shuffling forwards to see, their fear forgotten. Close enough to recognise her. Close enough to feel her effect.

She's madness, SixJen thought. *She's love and she's chaos and that's normal.*

But she's hate too. She's hate and she's venom.

The fugitive knelt through it all. Watching. Still smiling. Letting them touch her, when the mass boiled close. Letting

114

them press bloody lips and sweaty faces to her cheeks, her forehead.

'Freedom to do what the fuck we want!' someone yelled, balls deep in someone else. One of the cops, black and blue but happy, had joined in.

Madness.

The fugitive was lost to sight. Buried. Swamped. Taken into the mass like a sacrament to herself.

SixJen the killer reached out with her one remaining hand, shaking, sticky, sick with bloodloss, retching on air, and took up her gun. Tried to focus. Her eyes wouldn't stay still. Sweating heavily. Lips hanging. *Greyworld colourworld greyworld colourworld.*

She lifted the weapon with slow caution. And started shooting.

Nine

The panic invaded and insulated. Filled the air. Filled his mind.

Whatever holy mystery informed Teesa's weird influence on the kids around them, it was evidently no stronger than their more prosaic sense of self-preservation. The spell shattered the moment the mercenary-woman opened fire.

Sparks boiling. The world shaking to every shot.

Myq struggled to his feet amidst it all, shoved and shunted, snotting blood down his chin and chest, eyes watering, and tried to work out what the hell was going on.

The one-handed woman was shooting at the sky. Blood seething from her ruined wrist and across the floor. He remembered, guiltily, thinking her strikingly attractive in the crazy instants before he was knocked out: coffee brown, fastidiously hairless, features finely-printed but dead. Dead in all respects except the minor matter of being Alive.

Like a robot, he'd thought.

Not now. Now she was ashen, gloss-browed, eyes heavy and limbs limp. *Blood loss,* he figured. And weirdly, as if whatever numbing drug she'd taken (*what else could it be?*) had flushed clear through her open wound, now she was transformed. Fierce-eyed, snarling, firing into the ceiling with chin forward and teeth flashing. Spittle on her lip. Sweaty-faced.

Hot, Myq thought. Then hated himself.

She was clearing the room, that was obvious. Even through her grimaces, thinking tactically. Not aiming *at* but aiming *to* – to terrify the kids, to blast them back to sense, to send them scampering for the door.

To open a path to—

Tee.

She wants Tee.

Myq piled into the maul without thinking. Even with the carapace of horny flesh dissipating from the outside, Teesa was buried deep, a crush of limbs and shoes and sequins, of stinking scents and rolling eyes, and Myq found her only by flashes of her hair – silken black, discernible from the peacock-heads around it.

He hauled her out. He drew her from the crush like a survivor from wreckage and barely felt the effort. He dragged her – *her,* giggling; *her,* coiling arms round him; *her,* crooning his name; *her,* high on herself – back from the crowd, back from the killer, keeping the shrieking kids between them. Dragged her behind the bar, towards a service door, into the maw of a strip-lit corridor, out, out, *out.*

Only when he was halfway through the aperture, inured by jangling focus to the roaring weapon behind him, only then did it occur that all his thoughtless machismo, all his adrenal strength, all his uncharacteristic decisiveness, was predicated at least as much upon his seething jealousy at Tee sharing herself amongst all those writhing little shits – *mine! mine!* – as upon the tawdry matter of sparing her from impending execution.

'Myq?' Teesa said. A weird note to her voice. 'Myq, look.'

He stopped. Let her regain her feet. Glanced back.

Someone had got the front door open. The club, like

some clumsy decompression rendered in lurching slow-mo, was emptying all at once. And through the pack? Unblinking in the gaps between?

Her.

Standing alone. Yes, hunched and shaking, yes weak, yes grim … but still standing. Still enduring. Still refusing to stop. Strobes bombarding her. Smoke machines wreathing her in colour.

No words. No sneered commands. She simply stared as the stampede thinned, gun gripped ungainly beneath the shoulder of her useless arm, magazine angled open, slotting fresh flechettes into its breach without shifting her eyes.

No panic. No mistakes.

Reloading.

'Go,' Myq said. 'We haven't got long. Go go go go go g—'

'Myq.' He felt Tee's fingers on his cheek, felt his head being gently twisted. Her amber eyes pinning him to the spot. 'Myq, she'll follow. She won't stop.'

'But—'

'Myq. I love you.'

Something fell out from the bottom of Myqel's world. Something clouded his eyes and eked a current into his blood. Something removed his hands from her waist. Something swivelled his body away from her, back to the nightclub. Something squared his shoulders and set him, solid, in the doorway of the exit.

'Go,' he said, fully intending the gravelly heroic tone the situation demanded; in fact hitting an undignified note of petulance.

She kissed the back of his neck, maybe. He couldn't be sure. She leaned past and fired the laser twice – maybe. He wasn't really paying attention. She hit a couple of fleeing

118

kids, maybe, who went down all limbs and meat-smoke. Maybe. Chuckled once. Maybe. It all seemed a little abstract.

She loves me.

And then she was gone.

And then just emptiness, and lights flickering. And the merc.

Striding. Sudden. Dapple-lit.

'Move.'

He shook his head. Laughed like an idiot. 'Mine!' he shouted. 'She's mine!'

The merc curled a lip and lowered a shoulder. Didn't stop. Stumbled just once and barrelled, clumsy, into his side, apparently imagining she could shove past without resistance.

Mmmine!

She rebounded. Shock-faced. And then simply dropped – dropped slithering to the floor, bleeding out. Hissing like a dead balloon.

'Y-you okay?' Myq heard himself blurt. Stooping to help her on instinct, then jarring to a halt at the shimmering ridiculousness of it all, hand still outstretched. The merc simply blinked, staring up, eyes fluttering. As if, he guessed, confused at her own weakness. Fumbling again at her gun with an unsteady hand.

He slowly withdrew his arm.

'Um.'

'Do you know …' the woman said, sweat dripping in her eyes, gun lodged once more in her armpit. Breach snapping open. 'Do you know why she came here?'

'I …' Myq coughed politely into a fist. 'No. No, I don't really need to.'

'The man. The. The man who used to own her. Y-years ago. He was a trader.'

119

'Thank you, _yes_. Yes, I'm aware of that. If it's all the same to you, please just be qu—'

'A shibboletti trader.'

He chewed his lip. Suspecting weirdly that he should be making the most of this moment; that he should be kicking in the damaged woman's head and running like lightning.

But he didn't move. Couldn't.

'Did you know …' the merc said, shaking hand plucking at her own chest, fiddling with something gloss-gleaming and tiny. 'D-did you know that the price of … of shibboletti glands has increased f … four hundred percent … since your little stint killing freighters?'

'I …' He flopped his mouth open and shut. 'No. No, I did not.'

The woman dropped something into the breach of the gun. Snapped it closed with a sigh, then nodded. Exhausted.

'Well, it has.'

And then she shot him.

Later, after the rush and the escape, as the medbots of the _Shattergeist_ plucked and poked at his flesh, later he would discover through the fog of anaesthetics and hormostimms that the wound was barely more than superficial: an exquisitely-placed deposit into the meat on the side of his left buttock. (The beauty of being shot in the arse, as Tee would later giggle, was that in space you never had to sit down.)

But in the moment? In the clanging silence and sharp smoke-stink of the moment, a spot of the old Falling Over Whilst Shrieking occurred. A spot of the old scrabbling to get up, of yelping at the pain, of flitting back and forth between outrage and agony, of fixating – even through all that – on the likelihood that the killer was, even then, stepping over him, stumbling onwards after her prize. And at that, at least, Myq felt a surge of triumph. The merc would never catch Tee now. He'd bought her all the time she needed.

Get to the 'Geist. Get out of here!

(*I love you too!*)

But when he forced his eyes open and tried to swim above the pain the merc hadn't moved. Too weak. Slumped against the inside of the bar, breathing heavy. Even as he watched she dug in a pocket and crammed a bright little stimm into her mouth. He almost asked if he could have one too.

You can still walk, idiot. Go.

Go go go.

'She's not what you think,' the woman said, when he was halfway up.

Don't listen. Go. Go.

'You think she … you think she's spontaneous. Makes it up as she goes. Because. Because she's supposed to be. D'you understand?'

'No.'

'Runner's meant to run. Make a scene. Blaze a glorious trail. Nothing else. No plans.'

Raving. Crazy with bloodloss. Ignore her. Just go.

'That's how it works. How … How it's always worked. Runner runs. Hunters hunt.' The woman turned away, spittle pendulous on her lip. And began slowly, painfully, to crawl back towards the dancefloor. 'Taken too long, this one. She schemes. All gone wrong. Sick. Sneaky. Has to. Has to be stopped. Victor takes the crown.' She abruptly groaned. 'All begins again. Life cycle.'

Wait – what?

('*What do you know,*' Myq heard Tee say, a ghostly recent memory peppered with the splattered remnants of star-rammed shibboletti, '*about life cycles?*')

'Hang on,' he blurted, addressing that fleeting memory as much as he did the bloody killer heaving herself away across the floor. 'What do you mean?'

But the merc wasn't listening. Muttering to herself. The early effects of the stimm blitzing her brain before her body could catch up. Soon, Myq supposed, she'd be upright, bleeding or not. Deadly again.

(*Go! Go!*)

But as he turned away she croaked one last instruction amidst the nonsense – 'Culex …? Tell him. Tell him what she's done. And the … the King by the Lake. *Tell him.*'

The last Myq saw of her, before stumbling into the drizzling drear, the mercenary was poised over the unconscious body of the FIA agent, methodically cutting his throat with a razor-edged flechette. And whispering a word he couldn't hear.

Tee picked him up half a mile down the swampy access strip the repairs-crew had cut through the jungle. Hazy sensory signals, powerfully confounded by the relentless arse pain, birthed dreamlike impressions in the gaps between his memories. He recalled a phalanx of whining shapes hovering above the jungle; a tumbling squad of dainty cop-skimmers firing flak at something obscene and pink; a tinny voice too muffled to hear, calling his name; explosions amidst the spore clouds; a bright rainbow-chute descending from above to claw him up into the sky … and then darkness and loud music and a familiar voice laughing.

'I got shot in the arse,' he mumbled.

'Poor baby,' she said, typing something into the console. 'Wanna fuck?'

And then it stopped.

Just stopped. Ground down by queasy inertia and burnout one lazy afternoon on Baltha'Sine Station, two days later.

There was no warning that it would (none that Myq had detected, anyway). No sense – for him – of a destination being reached, a death-rattle coming to its end. The chase, the rampage, the momentum; all of it simply paused – as it had before on a dozen repair stops, a hundred refuellings, a thousand gory lacunae to watch their victims disintegrate (then transmit the footage to the news 'casters). It paused, but for the first time it did not resume.

Dragged to a halt by the party to end all parties, a hangover like an invidious bioweapon and, above all else, Myq's own simple arrival at a moment in which he had a little extra time to think.

'*Too late*,' Teesa mumbled in her sleep, turning over in the next room. '*Where are they …?*'

Hunched on an airfloat (arse still too sore to sit conventionally), Myq peered glumly round their berth – third spinward spoke, VIP suite, angled (according to long spacer tradition) onto the docking bay containing the *Shattergeist,* in all its vile-pink, grunting-honking-farting-shitting shibboletti-filled cargo-podded glory – he smoked a restorative vapourbrand and sighed. He could still taste the wretched creatures' whiff at the back of his throat after two days in transit.

It's over, Myq thought. *It's over and I don't know why.*

Thinking back to the saturnalian insanity of their arrival celebration, he liked to pretend he'd detected that subtle shift in pace the very moment they'd airlocked-in. But no. The truth was, as semiclads and nonclads alike had come swarming forth from the waiting crowd with flower garlands and banners, as the security guards they'd hired in advance (his idea) took up position, as cameradrones flickered and fruity punch flowed, as the party got underway like some great doomsday engine, Myq had magically intuited not a single notion of the dawning end. Had thought of nothing, in fact, except surrendering himself entirely to the adoration of the people.

Here, after all, was fame. *Here* was the notoriety he'd craved his whole life. The people of Baltha'Sine had greeted him and his lover like young gods.

Of course (he now told himself, consciously dialling down his own self-importance) it wasn't as though Baltha'Sine was a particularly well-appointed receptacle for celebrity. Home to only two million or so souls, the great cartwheel-city was part of neither the Federation (whose teeming masses he'd yearned to seduce, back when his ambitions were first overspilling their bounds), nor any of the other big factions. And yet to Myq's mind it was almost uniquely appointed as a cosmic weather vane: a place of cultural crosswinds and magpie-snatched influences.

Baltha'Sine sat at a territorial junction where the piece-meal borders of the Empire, the Federation and the Alliance succumbed to a diplomatic no-fly zone: a place where products and resources deemed too risqué or restricted by one faction could be quietly shuffled to another. The station had its own gloriously disinterested cops (whose principal role appeared to be politely informing outside agencies that their jurisdictions were *back that way*) and an exceedingly short list of laws. It was a place where adventurous students could spend a few years then forget to go home; to which artists could gravitate and piss away all their enthusiasm; where the cheerfully maladjusted could become invisible.

Accordingly its residents were almost pathologically open-minded: harvesters and hoarders of every idea, practice, imagery, religion, fashion, obsession, technology, entertainment, rumour, drug and deviancy which bubbled into the top layer of taboo from all three of the Main Galactic Players.

And on Balatha'Sine – on this perfectly formed acid-test for one's own importance – it turned out that Myquel Dobroba Pela-LeSire LeQuire and Teesa#32A[M/Tertius], were the obsession *du jour*. The mayor had even indulgently paused the station's centrifugal sections for a couple of hours (causing several thousand drinks to be messily liberated from their glasses) solely to stop Myq's buttock from twinging.

(The memory of that relief, typically, started up the ache again. He adjusted himself on the air-cushion and absently rattled the little translead pot the *'Geist'*s autodoctor had presented him, containing the projectile it'd dug out. He'd tried impressing a few strangers with it at the party – *I got shot, you know* – but the lumpy missile inside looked more like a button than an excitingly pointy bullet, and people were generally too blitzed to care.)

The madness had raged for twelve hours. The comedown, alas, looked set to last considerably longer.

'Wherrrre ...' Teesa whispered again.

And there was the problem. It was as if she'd simply and suddenly exhausted whatever reserve of ... of *whatever it was* ... that had been driving her. As if her endurance of the past months, her boundless energy and capacity for enthusiasm, her oscillating moods and mercurial rages, in fact all the relentlessness which defined her (which had somehow modulated from impossibility to normality in the short time they'd known each other) had sputtered and died.

'No no no no no no,' she whispered quietly from the bed, smacking her lips.

125

Not to put too fine a point on it, Myq found himself thinking clearly for the first time in weeks.

He thought – or rather, he *had* thought – that he knew the cause of the sudden arrested momentum. Before the party hit full stride, before the first Teesa-confuddled kids started getting naked, before even the first dance/fight got underway in the station's central plaza, the Mayor had nervously pulled them aside to make an announcement.

'He's … he's not here,' the dumpy woman had said with an air of fretful confession, wringing her tattooed hands.

'Who?' Myq blurted. Noticing only afterwards that Teesa was already reacting: lower lip jutting, a philosophical nod.

'Well … Axcelsus,' the Mayor said, as if it were obvious. 'The shibboletti trader. He *is* why you're here?'

Oh, oh, oh. It all came out like pus from a wound. Myq stumbling his way through it, planting questions with all the casual indifference his splintering dignity could manage. *Well, of course that's why we're here, yes, of course, of course, hahaha, so he's, he's gone, has he? How, uh, how long's he been here? When did he leave?* All while Teesa avoided eye contact and said nothing.

Madrien Axcelsus. The same Imperial slave-owning, super-wealthy prick from whom she'd first escaped. The one she'd shot in the back as she left. *Don't ask, don't ask.* A trader famed for his importance to the shibboletti-gland game, who – it transpired – had been one of Baltha'Sine's biggest sharks for the past few months, trading under the depressingly awful assumed identity of 'G. Lander'.

In that sticky moment Myq finally twigged. He hadn't wanted to, hadn't asked to, had in fact consciously prevented himself from digging too deep, not daring to risk the discovery there was something mundane behind their quest.

Vendetta.

It's all a bloody vendetta.

He'd grimly pieced it together with a feeling akin to falling. *She drives up the prices of shib' glands.* (She'd checked them, he remembered, when they first landed on Shibboleth.) *She knows Axcelsus's trading name from the Old Days. She announces a now-priceless cargo of live shibboletti* (the very message she was typing when she rescued him outside the club, for NoGod's sake), *and waits to see who bites.*

Inviting interested traders to bid.

Axcelsus.

This whole … fucking … thing… just to coax him out of the woodwork.

It was almost heartbreakingly tawdry. And, worse, the men and women of Baltha'Sine had worked it all out long before dumb, deliberately ignorant Myq had given it a thought. It was embarrassing, it was disappointing, it was bloody depressing. And it wouldn't even have the benefit of success.

'When … when we knew you were coming,' the Mayor had warbled, 'we tried to put him in custody. We thought we could … we could present him as a gift.' She distractedly rubbed herself along one thigh. 'But he was already gone. I'm so sorry. We've got a trace on him heading for the Empire – I mean, he would. He's very well connected. But … But please, don't leave. Not just yet. We're so excited to have you.'

And they were. And they'd showed it last night, even though between every cocktail and stimmstick – or the first few anyway – he was floundering with the fresh knowledge, with the almost unbearable need to take Tee aside to demand answers. And contending, all along, with the equally unbearable determination not to think about it. To bathe in the adoration and Let That Be Enough.

127

After all, Tee didn't seem that fussed. It was strange. She'd clearly reacted to the news, a stoic *hmm*, but no more. And almost as soon as the mayor released them back into the throng it was gone, forgotten, lost in the fun and the flirting.

And *ohhh*, she'd loved him so hard. She'd said it a dozen times in one night, after all these months of laughing it off. She'd touched nobody else. She'd clung to him as they smiled and danced and basked, and wherever they went people loved one another; hurt one another; shouted and fought and fucked and *lived*. And *she* was *his* alone.

He glanced back at her now – snoozing. Only the shifting of the quilt to say she was alive. He watched her little face and thought of the kids she'd killed in the nightclub, the man she'd glassed (to rousing cheers) last night, the cop she'd immolated above Shibboleth, the truckers' bodies popping against the hull off the shoulder of #A5FFP, the little journalist flopping dead like a boneless thing.

She's not what you think. The mercenary had said that. *She's not what you think.*

He dreamily opened the translead pot: a sudden determination to hold the bullet. Its lightness surprised him, glossy smooth and almost perfectly unthreatening. He strummed it once or twice, like a plectrum for the guitar he used to pretend-play when he was in the band, and sniffed. A bubble of dejection scrolling upwards along his spine.

'You're an idiot,' the bullet told him.

Myq had already snapped 'No, I'm not,' before he realised he'd gone insane. It felt weirdly overdue and perversely comforting.

'Here's a thing,' the button-projectile said – its voice miraculously contriving to soothe and annoy all at once. 'Did you ever ask her how old she is?'

'You're talking.'

'I repeat my original assertion. You're an idiot.'

'Right.' *Go with the flow*, he figured. *So you're mental. At least you'll never be lonely again.* 'No, actually. I never asked how old she is. Why?'

'Do me a favour? Switch on the console there. I can etherlink no problem, but you've got to let me in.'

'You're a bullet. Or a … a button. Or something.'

'I'm a Voight-Comal C-902 Culex-line Personal Companion. And you continue to be an idiot.'

Myq sputtered gently, for safety. The word *Culex* felt weirdly significant, even amidst the headachey thunder-heads and *delirium tremens*. Something the dead-eyed merce-nary had said as he'd staggered away from her?

The King by the Lake. Tell him.

Slowly, as if trying to prevent himself from noticing, Myq stretched out and sense-gestured at the console. It *oop*ed to life.

'Cheers,' the button said.

Instantly images began to cycle across the curtain-screen. Most were grainy – clearly captured by cheap surveillance cameras or the rudimentary sensors of humblebots – but the scenario throughout was clear: a lavish estate on some tropical world, a fire bubbling from ornate embrasures, a set of bodies lined up, an obese youth in trader's furs crumpled at the foot of a stairwell.

And her.

Of course, her. Striding away. Moodily shadowed. Curling a lip while stealing into a shuttle. He almost smiled at the sight: she'd barely changed since. Her hair had been a tad longer, eyes a tad dryer, clothes cut in the simple nylinen of an indentured worker. But still her.

Still insane.

Myq realised with a sigh he didn't need to see this. Didn't want to.

'So what?' he said, keeping his voice low. *Don't want to wake her.* 'I know this story. You're, what ...? You're trying to tell me she's not an angel? Golly. I'm amazed. That's, yeah. That's really opened my eyes. I think I'll shit you out the waste-chute now, if it's all the same to you.'

'Idiot.'

'Look, I'm sure it's violating some sort of customer directive to keep calling me th—'

'Look at the timestamp, dummy.'

Myq sighed and squinted closer.

Then a little closer.

'That's. No, that's wrong.'

'It's not wrong.'

'But that's twenty years ago. The camera must've been fau—'

The little drone tutted. Cycled through a dozen images from the same scene – all whilst somehow radiating a sense of indulgent impatience – each of which confirmed that Teesa's bloody escape from the clutches of Madrien Axcelsus really was (*no, no, no, that's stupid*) two decades old.

'All right,' the little voice chirped. Enjoying itself. 'Revelation number two.'

A new image flashed up. A grim portrait: steeped in baroque pomposity and all the fiddly bric-a-brac of officialdom.

PILOTS' FEDERATION BOUNTY LICENCE, the over-designed title read. **SANCTIONED AGENT TERESA NINER.**

The face below was harsh-lit: flat-skinned and sallow. The hair had been shaved clean off, the cheeks hollow with malnourishment, and the eyes—

Fuck, no.

130

No, that's not her.

—the eyes were dead. As glimmer-free and loveless as either of those killers in the nightclub two days ago. It was the face of a warrior, the face of a destroyer; the face of a hunter.

Myq glanced back over his shoulder, as if to check the likeness.

'That's … that's Tee. How … how is that p—'

More screens. A cavalcade of press-shots and vid-captures. Gangsters, killers, pirates: a litany of badmen and enemy agents captured and killed, their cold-eyed nemesis avoiding the lens in each image. The scenes, altogether, spanned six years of violence.

Her, her, her.

But not her. A Robot-her. A bitter-her. A shadow-eyed joyless her.

'How?' he said, suddenly overwhelmed by a need to vomit. 'H-how's this … how did …'

'Thirteen years ago,' the little button said, 'which is seven years after the thing with Madrien Axcelsus, right? Seven years after she escaped and became a merc. Thirteen years ago that woman killed a guy. A criminal. A fugitive. I don't have any photos of him and his name doesn't matter. What matters is that almost instantly she underwent a change.'

'I … I don't—'

'Over the next thirteen years, up to now, she … well, she destroyed stuff. That's about the size of it. She ran. Spun from one chaotic little act to another. All pretty lowkey to start with – nothing you'd call exciting. But … building up. Becoming a fugitive in her own right, after all those years chasing 'em. And leaving little outbreaks of … of promiscuity wherever she went. Of motiveless crazy. Ohhh,

131

every now and then someone'd show up to try to kill her, sure … but she ran and she ran and she ran and nobody ever quite managed.

'And that's how it was, Myq-the-idiot—'

'I *said* stop c—'

'—until a few months back, when some cops on Gateway – so off-their-heads on performance stimms and overtime they barely even felt that creepy influence your missus has on people, and don't look at me like that, you know what I mean – they arrested her for disturbing the peace. Ran her prints. Came up with some extremely fucking elderly outstandings. And then, ha, the cherry on the crapcake that was their night – pulled in a pissed-up celeb on the same charge. Rest's history.'

'But—'

'*But but but.* But! Twenty years, Myq. Didn't age a single day in that whole bloody time.'

Myq felt a sigh go out of him like a ghost. A long *hhhhhh* which modulated, without conscious thought, into a broken-voiced '*How?*'

The little bead seemed to shiver in his hand.

And said, 'Nemorensis, mate.'

The screens died. Myq blinked, lost, floating. 'What's … what's Nemorensis?' he croaked.

And a soft voice behind him said, 'How do you know that word?'

He almost fell off the air-cushion. Twisted too hard, bashed his arse against the edge of the console and howled a storm. All of which, luckily, concealed the extremely-bloody-obvious Guilty Expression smearing his face like lipstick.

'Um,' he said, holding his arse. 'You're up then?'

Teesa smiled. Didn't mean it.

132

'That word?'

The little robot piped-up on cue. 'It's just something that crazy weird woman in the nightclub said. Right? Right before shooting you.'

'Er,' Myq said.

'Don't worry, she can't hear me.'

'But—'

'I'm resonating a sonic cone against the cartilaginous elements of your ear. It's very clever.'

(*So what you're telling me,* Myq carefully didn't say, didn't break down in hysterical overfrazzlement to shout, *is that you're a voice in my fucking head?*)

'It's just something,' he mumbled, 'that crazy weird woman in the nightclub said. Before she shot me in the arse.'

Teesa's smile turned genuine. Her eyes glittered. 'Huh. Mental.'

'I know!'

Smile, smile. Laugh, laugh. Kiss, kiss.

'You … you feeling okay, then?' he ventured, feeling his cheeks burn. Facial and buttockal.

'Perfect. Why?'

It's just that you've been awake for fifteen seconds and you haven't tried to fuck me yet.

It's just that you're an escaped-slave dead-eyed mercenary crazy-mental genocidal maniac in her mid fifties. And I'm basically terrified of you.

Also, I have an erection.

And I love you so much.

'No reason.'

'Nebular. Okay. So, listen. I'm going to nip across to the *Shattergeist*.'

'What for?'

133

'The shibboletti, silly! Poor things've been sitting there in that horrid old cargo pod for two days without a bite to eat. That's just plain cruel.'

'R-right.' He fiddled with the buttonbulletrobot. *Guilty, guilty, guilty.* 'You … you want some company?'

('Stay where you fucking are,' the little computer tweeted.)

'No, no. You stay here, my poor wounded soldier.' She slapped him playfully on the arse. He manfully turned his shriek into a chuckle. 'And Myq?'

'Mm?'

'I love you, Myq. You remember that.'

'I … I love you too.'

'I mean it.' She leaned down again. Kissing him with a curious precision. 'Don't forget it.'

And then she was gone.

Over, Myq thought. Tears quite suddenly prickling in his eyes. *Over, and I don't know why.*

'Do you want to know,' the robot said, 'what Nemorensis means?'

Ten

Eventually, of course, the pain died away.

Always does, Sixjen thought – almost sad. *Always will.*

Yes, true, the *The*'s autosystems had dutifully pumped her with a banquet of anaesthetics the second she'd crawled back onboard, and a second course of the same while tidying her mangled wrist, dumbly monotoning its bedside reassurances: *all over soon, best you don't look.*

(So different, she'd reflected, from Lex's affected eccentricities. It was astounding that two machines, neither more alive than the other, could present such extremes of companionship.)

But no, it wasn't the drugs. Ultimately the pain was sent packing by the simple regrouping Numbness of her condition: that old apathy, that old swaddling-layer of chilly armour, re-infecting her as the hours passed.

Out here. Drifting. Far beyond the enlivening influence of the runner.

Out here the excitement curled and died. Out here the anxieties of the chase, the frustration at coming so close, the flush of triumph as she'd whispered the word and opened the FIA man from carotid to jugular … all of it melted away. All dissolved into greyness.

Why hasn't he called?

Only loneliness remained – and even then only the ghost of it – while the autosurgeon picked at atomised bone, while a chemical broth rinsed away the sad necrotic remnants of her hand, while a laser grid sealed the whole ungainly mess at the wrist. For a while she regretted giving up Lex so easily. (He would've made a joke by now, she clumsily imagined, about pirates. *Get a hook, boss.* Instead: silence.)

But even the regret, in time, sputtered out. The darkness of the cockpit, the endless void beyond: it seemed to soothe away all external concerns. What could be grander than the emptiness, after all? What could stand against it? What could impotently proclaim its relevance, set before that?

Only the hunt. Only the chase. Those old imperatives, slamming back.

She'd exhausted the limits of her investigative logic early on, too. It had been clear since the episode at Tun's Wart – since that secret flicker of recognition on the runner's face (*sad eyes, sad eyes*) – that the fugitive was circling inexorably towards her old owner: poor, crippled Madrien Axcelsus. Although whether that was to enact some overdue revenge or to persecute further the man she'd already so damaged, or simply to give her pursuers some obtuse aid in their pursuit, SixJen couldn't say. The trip to Shibboleth and the pickup of a livestock herd tallied with all of the above at any rate: a trail of breadcrumbs to follow. A bundle of bait to draw out the trader.

And yes, sure enough, in the hours after the runner's escape from Shibboleth an anonymous marketplace bulletin had been scattercast across the grid, advertising the availability of a veritable *fortune* in fresh shib' glands.

Them. Definitely them.

But Madrien Axcelsus hadn't traded under his own name in the decades since Teesa first escaped him. SixJen knew that – had known it for years. And like him, amidst the welter of trader bids offered against the advertised livestock, almost all of the others used false titles or umbrella business-fronts. Glanders were not, by inclination, a straightforward breed, and if indeed Axcelsus was amongst the names registering bids he might have been any one of them. SixJen had to assume Teesa, with all her years in his service, knew which it was.

She, SixJen, alas did not. *Clever little cow.*

(*The runner's not supposed to scheme!*)

No point bemoaning it. And no chance, now, of feeling the frustrations she supposed she should. Instead? Instead for a day and a half SixJen the killer had simply sat. Nowhere in particular. A couple of jumps clear of Shibboleth; a scoop-stop to refuel. Then nothing.

Waiting.

Why hasn't he called?

When it came, that gentle chime against the edge of her senses, her first thought was that she was imagining it. That happened, sometimes. Echoes, she supposed, of the person she once was (*the Autumn Villa … the stink of burnt chocolate …*) smuggling out like coils of smoke from the safebox she'd become.

Besides, she was so accustomed to Lex dutifully alerting her to the prosaic functions of her environment – *we got a call coming in, chief* – that it briefly made more sense for the tinny tone to originate in her own brain than the ship. And even when she'd pulled herself together and manually opened the line, the confusion remained: Lex's annoying nonsense filling the cockpit as if nothing had happened.

'Got a special someone wants a word, boss,' he said. 'Also, did you eat yet today? You should eat.'

She bit down on the urge to tell him off. Then did the same with a relief-filled greeting; defaulting to businesslike instead:

'Is this line secure? Where are you?'

'Runner's not here, if that's what you mean. Just me and the rock star, boss. And he says ... he says if I tell you the "where" he'll dump me down the shitchute and be gone in ten.'

'He thinks I give a damn about you?' (*I do. I do. I do.*)

Lex affected an offended cough. 'That's, *uh.* That's what I told him. But – sorry, sorry – I also told him you still owe two hundred kay to that guy you bought me off, what was his name, "Pullzine"?, something like that—' (SixJen scowled: *what?*) '—and so I assured him you wouldn't risk it.'

'I see.'

I don't see.

Pullzine. Pullzine. Pullzine. I don't owe anyone anything. Who or what is Pullz—

'Anyway, he just wants to talk.'

SixJen wobbled her jaw, brain racing. 'Visual?'

'Sure. Very shortwave. Won't be much cop, quality wise.'

'Fine.'

'You ... uh. You presentable, boss?'

'Just do it.'

'The control's at your end. Sorry. Adjacent to the software directory. Big red button, mistress. Right there.'

She blinked. *Mistress? He doesn't talk like this.*

Trying to tell me s—

'You see it, ma'am?'

Ah.

Yes. Yes, she saw it.

Oh Lex. You clever little thing.

The software directory. A dull list of the *The*'s constantly-running operational programs, holocurtained at the fringe of her liminals. Most items had thoroughly unimaginative names – *LifeSuppTech*, *OxySys* – but lurking innocuous among them, marked by the fussy skull logo of an open-source pirate program, she saw it: **PullZine Tracer**. One of the suite of maybe-useful-oneday apps she'd given Lex carte blanche to purchase.

Clever little pretend-brain. Clever little fakelife.

She stabbed at the execution command—

[SIGNAL TRACE RUNNING. STANDBY.]

—and took a deep breath. Opened the visual channel.

And said, 'Hello Myquel.'

The boy … the boy looked broken.

SixJen could not, in all honesty, claim a talent for empathy. But even to her cold eyes, poring across his expression as if strategising over a chessboard, Myquel Dobroba Pela-LeSire LeQuire looked like a man whose faith had been fucked by an axe.

'Lex showed you the footage, then?' she intuited.

He nodded, just once. He put her in mind of a cornered rodent: undecided as yet whether to run or play dead, but unhappily aware neither would work.

'What … what *is* she?' he said. 'Teesa.'

SixJen turned on a smile – a calculated attempt at reassurance – then switched it back off. *It makes people nervous*, Lex had told her once.

'On old Earth,' she said, 'in a forgotten country, on the shore of a lake named *Nemi*, there was a myth. You understand myths, Myq?'

He nodded, scowling. 'I understand *legends*,' he said, more pointed than she'd expected. He kept glancing over his shoulder.

On the holo beside his image a progress bar began to creep towards a graphic marked 'signal traced'. It was, SixJen noted, painfully long.

139

'It's a myth about a priest,' she said. 'A Holy King, in fact. Lap of luxury. All the power and prestige you could want. That's a comfortable job, Myq. A good gig, yes? Apart from a few minor details.'

Nod. Nod. Barely listening. Sweat on his brow.

'One: you could only get this job by killing your predecessor. And two: you could only quit the job by being killed.

'This priest? He was *Rex Nemorensis*: the King by the Lake.'

'I ... don't see what this has to do w—'

'It's a cover. It always was. All the ritual and the religion. The chase through the forest. The final fight. The new incumbent clambering up to break off a golden bough to prove his worth. It's all set dressing, Myquel. All fluff to hide something stranger. Something people couldn't – or wouldn't – believe.'

'Like what?'

'But you won't believe it either. That's the point.'

'Just ... just tell me, okay. I shouldn't be talking to you. Just hurry up and tell me.'

'Is she *there*, Myq?'

'That's none of your business.' Another glance over his shoulder.

Good. SixJen nodded. *She's near.*

'Imagine ...' she waved her hand, mock-breezy. 'Imagine a creature made of thought. No, imagine a *race* of them. Little invisible beasts. They make no sense if you're thinking biologically. You have to be ... more abstract.'

'Fine. Whatever. So what?' Trying his best to be unflappable. Failing.

'These creatures ... they live inside people's brains. Particular people. Very specific people. They take them over and they change them. And one way they do that, Myq, is they make them stop getting older. Like Teesa. And like me.'

140

He blinked at that. Crazily orbiting eyes flicking up to stare straight down the lens.

'You too?' Voice quiet.

'I'm almost fifty,' she shrugged. And took the opportunity, while he chewed that down, to glance aside. The progress bar was passing 40%.

'So … why you?' he said, eventually. 'Why her? Which "specific people", exactly?' His tone was beginning to spike with scorn. 'And how come nobody knows about all this?'

Too much to hope, she supposed, *he'd swallow it easy.*

'These creatures … they live inside slaves. Escaped slaves, to be precise. That's how it was, back by the lake – that's how it is now. I don't know why. Maybe they're drawn to … what? To minds familiar with powerlessness. Minds which understand freedom, something like that. Minds that'll do anything to escape.'

Myq's eyes went suspicious. 'So … you were a sl … You were like Teesa? Before?'

She nodded, just once. And then almost cried out, almost lost herself, in the flock of images that bustled up and screeched around her.

The factories!

The merthiq leaves falling for second Autumn … the men in purple coming to trade, to buy, to switch and swap the stock. Money passing from tablet to tablet: contactless life-exchange. Future decided by transactional 'blip!'

(How long, she wondered, since she'd last thought these thoughts?)

'New meat for the Villa,' one said, sneering.

And oh, her mother, crying (her mother! she'd had a mother!). *The foreman shouting, 'Back to it, back to it!', and the steam and the machines and …*

And the landtrain whining.

141

And the villa growing in the distance. And the laughter of men and the glimmering of eyes and that … sinking … feeling.

Fourteen.

She was fourteen when they sent her to the fuckshop.

'Yes,' she said. Not a tremble in her voice. Not a curl to her lip. (*Screaming inside!*) 'I was a slave. Imperial core-world Topaz, in the Facece system. I escaped during a minor riot aged thirty-five. I'd already been on the run six months when the … the creature came into me.' She tapped her head and swallowed, throat unexpectedly dry. 'That was thirteen years ago.'

Thirteen.

Years.

Of waiting.

Myq breathed out all at once. As if the spell, along with his credulity, had broken apart at the very cusp of completion.

'This is … look, sorry, this is stupid.' A miniature tantrum shifting across his brows. 'I just … all I want is to know how come she's in those photos and … and why you won't leave us alone. That's all.'

'I'm trying to explain.'

'But it's insa—'

'Myquel, it's not that I won't leave her alone. Try to understand. It's that I can't. No more than she could stop doing what she does.'

Running.

Exulting.

(She's not supposed to plan!)

The trace, SixJen noticed – almost forgotten in the acrid bloom of those age-old memories – was shuffling past 60%.

'These creatures,' she said, ignoring Myq's huff, his proto-eyeroll, 'these living thoughts … these things … There are

142

thirteen. Never more. Twelve of them are the Aspirants. Or the … the hunters, if you like. Twelve who live to chase. Circling and circling the thirteenth. We call her the runner because that's how the game plays out, these days. Out here in the stars it's far more of a chase than a duel. Do you see? That's the only way it can work. But it's the same as in that myth, Myq. The King by the Lake.

'She is the Rex Nemorensis. And she has to die.'

'I-I don't see h … This is crazy. It's crazy.'

'Think of it as a mating ritual. Think of the chasers as … horny idiots. Males sniffing for a fuck.'

'You mean … You mean like you? You're male?'

'Yes. Abstractly speaking. Or rather, the thing that lives in here is.' She rapped her stump against her temple. 'Same as that man in the nightclub. Same as all the others.' Secretly, out of sight of the camera, she touched the fresh stump of her wrist to the puckered scars along her left arm. It hadn't been easy, adding fresh ones. It had taken time and care and a knife carefully clamped by the auto-surgeon – against its bleated protests. But she'd done it. The final four. The FIA man and the three he'd already claimed.

Eleven scars: *No. More. Competition.*

'All they can think about, these males, is catching her. It's all they are, Myq. I said it before: they're living ideas. Conceptual life. Truly alien. And the funny part is,' (*it's not funny*), 'they didn't come from up here, in the stars. They were with us all along.'

Myq wiped at sweat. Glanced round as if hunting for an escape. SixJen juggernauted blithely on – noting the tracer at **[87%]** – refusing to break the flow.

'Now these males?' she said. 'They're more like … incomplete ideas. They're dull and they're dead and there's no room, Myq, *no room*, for anything in their poor little souls

143

except desire. They want … they *need* … to be completed. And for that they need her.'

The boy quite abruptly stopped moving. Eyes finally still. Fixed on hers.

The first traces, she was sure, of belief. Of horror.

And (*oh, poor boy*) of jealousy.

He wants her all to himself.

(On her seventeenth birthday, SixJen remembered – *stop thinking, stop remembering, stop stop stop* – the consortium of young businessmen who owned her, all self-declared VIPs with stupid haircuts and Latin-accent affectations, including the nephew of a senator and a Petty-General's ward, borrowed her from their own brothel as part of a deal sweetener with some visiting corporate sleazesuits. One of them, in a dark corner of a smoky boardroom, bit her so hard as he came that she needed stitches.

The deal collapsed in the shouting match that followed. It was the first time she remembered ever feeling important.)

Not a twitch on her face. Not a notion of the recall.

'But the female?' she said. 'The female *burns*. That's *her* living idea. She's … she's chaos and ecstasy and instinct. She infects. You've seen that, haven't you?'

Half a nod. He looked like he might cry.

'She consumes the world, Myq. It pours out of her. All the people you've seen … animals, plants. Screwing, fighting. That's how she feels *all the time*. We call it the Reward. And none of us … nobody can imagine how good it is.

'But here's the dichotomy … See, part of her wants it to go on and on forever. Always escalating. Always running. Always fucking, always fighting. That's the part, I think, you love. And you do love her, don't you Myq?'

As if a spell had been uttered, as if that one loaded word

144

were enough to tip him into an abyss, a single tear broke from his eye as he nodded.

'But the other part of her? Ohhh … that wants nothing more than to be mated. To be caught.'

The tracer chimed. She showed no reaction, barely sparing it a glance. **[SIGNAL TRACED.]** Astronavigational coordinates scrolling by. She slowly stretched out her left hand, her only hand – still clumsy with inexperience – and dialled a set of commands.

On screen the boy swiped to dry his cheek, a late flicker of defiance in his voice.

'Well, that's … that's where you're wrong. Teesa's fine as she is. Doesn't want to be … mated by anyone except me, thankyousoverymuch.'

The poor kid was actually blushing.

'You're thinking too mammal, Myq. That's not how it works. You've got to … to open your mind. There are some very strange life-cycles out there.'

A hint of a frown ghosted at his face. 'Life cycles …?'

'What's wrong?'

'It's …' Another slow tear. Another wipe. And there – deep in his eye – she saw it. The final mote of acceptance. 'I think she tried to tell me about this stuff herself,' he whispered.

'Oh?' SixJen pretended curiosity. Finger hovering above a control. 'What did she say?'

Myquel opened his mouth. Glanced away from the lens, staring off into the spaces of his memory. 'I-it was while we were splatting shibbolettis,' he began. 'She started going on ab—'

SixJen hit the control. The *The* pulsed around her. An oily lurch, a greasy static stroking its way into the air. FTL, she'd heard, often brought with it a curious sense of

145

detachment: a spooky separation of the self from the self. But to a victim of such profound psychic constipation as her, travelling through witchspace felt strangely like the physical sensation of weightlessness, albeit applied abstractly to thoughts.

The rush ended. The stars re-aligned. The vidscreen, which had flickered with a succession of eerie intermediates, restored Myquel's grainy image as if nothing had happened.

'—d all types of weird wildlife,' he was saying. 'I ... I didn't give it much thought at the time, but ... but maybe she was trying to let me know.'

'You could be right,' SixJen said, congratulating herself inwardly. The computer diligently began re-charging the drives, a new nav-solution clattering across the holo.

One more jump. Keep him talking.

'Listen very carefully,' she said. 'For these creatures, Myq ... like the one I've got and the one she's got. For our lifecycle? Fucking means dying.'

(In her late twenties ... little-by-little the customers stopped picking her from the line-up. *Don't think about it.*

You know what's coming. Stop it.

Aged thirty-one, the owners moved her to a room at the back of the villa. '*Personal use only,*' they told the madame. '*Take her off the market.*'

Aged thirty-two (*stop it stop it*) she had her nose broken for the first time. Three fresh scars on her upper arm, thigh, chest.

Aged thirty-three she spent two months in a ward. A 'private party', they told the bored praetor-cops who came to investigate. Just the senator's nephew, five of his bestest pals, and a selection of blunt toys. No harm done.

Aged thirty-four (*stop it stop it stop it*), after her eighth

146

hospitalisation, after her fifth skin-graft, after her third abortion, they told her she'd be sent back to the factory. *All she's good for*, they said.

She dared to hope they were telling the truth. They weren't.

Aged thirty-five a minor revolt broke out at a nearby cocoa plantation. Nothing to do with her. Nothing to do with anyone. The brothel was invaded; almost an after-thought. The madame murdered. The senator's nephew and the general's ward strung from the merthiq trees outside as burning cocoa doused the world in sooty chocolate.

The rebelling mob was annihilated two days later.

She simply wandered away, forgotten. Nobody seemed to care much about an unwanted whore.

All she's good for.

All she's good for.

'Rex Nemorensis,' SixJen said, chewing down on the trembling in her legs (*pain from the hand, tiredness, adrenaline; that's all it is*). 'You don't get to be the priest unless you kill your predecessor.'

'I don't understand.'

'Whichever male kills the female, Myq? They become it.'

'That's ... that's ...'

'It's not mammal, no. Stop trying to understand. Maybe it's ... *oh*, maybe it's something to do with triumph. Moment of victory. Maybe that's what causes the jump. I don't know. But in that second ...? In that instant when the male whispers the word to open the way, when the female dies ... she shatters apart. Spills into space. Twelve new males – like holy spores, Myq – go swooping off to find a likely brain ... a scared little runaway slave ... to bond with.'

'This is insane.'

147

'Yes, it is. But in that second, the male who did it, Myq? The one who caught the runner … that male finds his – or *her*, or *hisher, or herhis, or its*, because we're past genders now, aren't we? Because this is *my* future we're talking about – that hunter finds their brain breaking apart too. The ecstasy pouring in. The holy reward.'

She could hear her own heart speeding just talking about it … and yet couldn't feel a thing. So she fixed the boy on the screen with a look fit to pin him to a page and said:

'Ask me the question, Myq.'

'What … What if … What if none of you kills her?' *Good boy.* 'What if she gets away? What if something *else* happens?'

'I don't know,' she smiled. And meant it. 'Honestly, I don't. It's never happened. Do you understand? All this … it's been going on for millennia. At the start … oh, it must have been so easy! The priest, right there! The wood, the lake. You knew where to find him. All you had to do was challenge.

'But the years've muddled it, haven't they? Travel. Expansion. Rationalism. About the only thing that didn't get in the way was the abolition of slavery on old Earth, because there's never been a shortage of minds which feel owned. That's what this whole thing's about, after all. About the way people feel. About ideas. About spreading yourself into as many brains as you can.'

[FTL DRIVE RECHARGED. STANDING BY___.]

'And every step we took out into the stars, Myq?' her hand, hovering again. 'Every time we expanded? Every time we multiplied and grew further apart … *touching people got harder.*'

Another tear on the boy's cheek. *A nerve.*

She held up a finger – or tried to, then waggled the stump regardless – and ratcheted up the smile, as if

148

presenting the good news to follow the bad. 'Luckily for us the runner's programmed to make a scene. Even across the span of the cosmos, she can't help but make a noise. It's just what she does.'

The boy sniffed. Swallowed hard. 'So. So all this? This smashing and crashing? This is all just ... just part of it?'

Meaning: *so I'm just the fluff?*

'I'm afraid so. Although ... there is one difference.' His head tilted back up. (*That's all he wants – to be special.*)

'This one, Myq. She doesn't just run. She plans. She schemes. She's ... she's vindictive.' She was worried he'd try to protest, but he didn't. Just nod, nod, nodded.

'She's toxic,' he muttered, staring at the floor.

He knew. He knew all along.

She hit the control. Hoping he wouldn't notice the view-screen flicker, so lost in his gloom. She felt the Universe shift around her again. Heart hammering like a distant noise.

(She'd stood there for half an hour, she remembered. As cocoa smoke spiralled and distant gunshots rang. Just staring at the bodies of those men: hanging. Turning with the breeze. The men who'd raped her, broken her, humiliated her. Owned her.)

She couldn't honestly say, now, what she'd felt during that time – too distant from the emotion; too separate from the lexicon of feeling. But she was sure of one thing: she'd felt no joy.

Unlike Teesa.

SixJen had seen the images. That bloody sylph, stalking away from the fire she'd set at the Axcelsus home. Sneering over the bodies of her fellow slaves.

The *The* dropped into reality on the edge of the Baltha'Sine system, and if Myquel had noticed the brief outage of Lex's uplink he gave no sign of it.

149

'She was broken from the start,' he muttered. 'Wasn't she?'

'I think so. She's … she's too good at it, Myq. Nobody's ever reigned by the lake this long. She's become … *nasty*. Sneaky. She's gained more enemies than any runner before. She's falling apart. She's insane. She's—'

'I get it.'

'No, you don't. She could do *anything*, Myq. She could destroy *herself*. What then?'

He bit his lip. Shook his head. 'She wouldn't do that.'

'How do you know? She's getting worse. You know this. She's working up to something. Something big.'

He was silent for a moment. Turned to glance back over his shoulder, as if an inkling of something were needling into his mind. A grim notion.

'What?' she said.

But he shook his head, talking himself out of it, and almost snarled. 'She … *No*, she just came here to find Axcelsus. That's all. Revenge against her bloody boss! It's … it's boring. But for fuck's sake that's all this is. He's not here, end of story.'

'Then why are you still there?' Far beyond the system's boundaries, the *The* turned silently towards the distant station. 'Wherever you are.'

'I …'

She could almost see the thoughts wrestling inside him. The systematic collapse of all he thought he knew.

'She loves me,' he whispered, pathetic. 'She said so.'

'She can't love. Nothing but the chase. Nothing but chaos.'

'But she *said*.'

SixJen felt an unexpected stab of impatience. She knew then that she was close. Too intoxicated by the emotion to

150

suppress it. 'Myquel! For fuck's sake, if she does something stupid! If she dies without me there ... this race ... this cycle ... it all ends too.'

He didn't care. She could see that. Wallowing. Turning on a spit of his misery.

'Thousands will die. Whatever she's planning. She's been building up all along. Don't you care about that?'

He didn't.

Or if he did it barely registered on the gauge of his need. 'We'll be famous,' he whispered. 'Whatever happens. Everyone will know.'

SixJen closed her eyes. Took a breath. And took a risk.

'Myquel. The chase will end. Forever. The rush will end. Do you understand? Is that what you want?'

The boy went deathly still. Eyes fixed. Brain spinning onwards in silence.

'I don't believe a word of this,' he snarled. Dismal. Lashing out without claws. 'Don't try to find us. We'll be long gone.'

He reached up. The visual died. The audio snapped inert.

I'm already here, you poor little idiot.

Eleven

He finally found her, moments before all his composted emotion and crushed-in panic bubbled into a fully-flung tantrum, in the great steaming mouthpiece of the *Shattergeist*'s cargo holds. Chuckling to herself.

There, where once Myq and the band had lazed in a luxurious tour-suite, where now serried rings of voidseals and electroclamp bulkheads gave from the ship's habitable foresections into the retrofitted cluster of produce-pods, batteries, generators, ammo-magazines and the other assorted add-ons they'd bought, Teesa stood proudly on what Myq had always considered, aesthetically, the ceiling. It felt somehow appropriate.

She's magic. She's insane. She's not human.

Of course *she's upside-fucking-down.*

As was Myq himself, to be fair, though for far less exotic reasons than the bloody-minded alien nonconformity his addled brain ascribed to Teesa. Still anchored by a doglegged docking-hook to the outer hub of Baltha'Sine Station, hence afflicted by the same gravity its centrifugal momentum faked, the *Shattergeist*'s normally directionless interior had become a weird landscape of mundane ups and downs, but never quite in the way the eye expected. All the ladders and double-sided walkways (which seemed so unnecessarily ubiquitous during weightless travel, forever getting in the way of a serene float-through or innocuous zee-gee bonk) suddenly became tiresomely vital. It had taken Myq twenty minutes just to clamber, scramble and hop his way down (up) to the cargo decks. Now sweating, panting, venting a thick air of brainbroken agitation – *aliens! Living ideas! Bullshit! Bullshit!* – he was in precisely no mood for Tee's giggly upside-down nonsense, even if he was technically oriented just the same.

'Where've you *been*?' he all but snarled.

His little chat with the bounty hunter, in hindsight, had not helped his zen.

'Saying hello to the fartybeasts,' she tittered, still poking at controls. 'They were lonely.'

Sure enough, from the central cargo-pod, the tumultuous honking and steaming stink of the shibboletti had increased a hundredfold. Myq missed a couple of heartbeats as it stole over him: the non-triumph of being right about a horrible suspicion.

She has plans ...

'Are they ... are they okay in there?' he said.

She just laughed. She was high, that was clear. Higher than usual, even: pupils huge against mossy irises. A thoughtless smirk kept invading her face while she concentrated, and yet the dark makeup round her eyes (pasted on so thick it reminded him abstractly of warpaint, applied in anticipation of ... of *whatever this is*) had run in streaks across her cheeks like the pinbones of a bat's wing. She'd been crying.

'You ... you want to tell me what's up?' he whispered; all his agitation, all his glum theories, all the paranoid notions seeded by the bounty hunter deflating at the sight of her. His erection, on cue, was already developing.

'Just turning off the shock absorbers,' she trilled, as if it was the sort of thing People Just Do.

'Why?'

153

'Silly. Because they absorb too much shock.'

'Which, ah ...' Myq scratched his head. He was feeling strangely breathless. (*The hunter was right, for NoGod's sake ... 'She's getting worse. You know this. She's working up to something.'*) 'Which is a problem because ...?'

Teesa just gave him a look. *Don't ask, silly.*

He nodded. *That's the way it's always been. Way it'll always be. Ask no questions, receive no lies.*

Stop stalling, idiot.

He took a ragged breath and reached for her shoulder. Kissed her twice on the skin of her neck, just below and behind her ear. Relishing the scent but fighting, wrestling, screaming inwardly, not to get lost in it. Running a hand across the fabric of her natty spacer-jacket then up inside the zip.

'Oh,' she said. Meeting his eyes. Arching a brow. 'Rrrreally?'

'Really.'

It was only when they were undressed, clinching, shivering a little in the chill air of the hold that he remembered the stimms he'd brought with him.

'I'm ... I'm tense,' he said, pretext-hunting. 'Cold. Let's just ... H-here. You want some?'

And did he imagine it? Did she pause for just a second before swallowing them? Fractionally wary?

But of course she'd never say 'no' to anything – he doubted she was capable – so she emerged from the hesitation to wolf them down with such gusto she didn't even pause to see if he was doing the same.

Which ... Well.

So they made love.

Slower, he thought, than usual. Maybe something to do with the novelty of gravity. Maybe the drugs acting on her quicker than he'd thought they would. Maybe just his own

154

soppy fucking interpretational stupidity, seeking romance at the end of the world. But yes, in the preferred narrative of his sentimental brain it was more than just a Slow Screw, it was *important* in ways it'd never been before. It was important and it was passionate and it was final, and it lacked all trace of the rote routine he'd (guiltily) sensed creeping into their rutting over the past weeks. They held one another with arms instead of hands. They rocked rather than thrust. They met with eyes at least as often as lips. They ran fingertips across backs and breasts and stared and explored and discovered. (Myq, for instance, had never noticed the shadow of several old medically-removed scars hidden beneath the noisy colour of her sleeve-tats, and almost blubbed at the possibility of there being other mysteries, other secrets, he'd never get the chance to unearth.)

And so there and then, without fear, without hesitation or vacillation, as shibboletti honked and stamped in the pod beyond them, he said it.

'Tell me.'

'Mm?'

'Tell me what you're doing, Tee. Tell me what this is all about. Tell me the plan.'

She smiled at him. Not quite able – *the drugs* – to keep her eyes still for long. 'You never asked before,' she said.

'I want to share now. I love you. I want to know.'

She stared at him for just a little longer than he would've liked, those unfocused eyes – those pools of weed-strewn whiskey – briefly sharp. Then she remembered herself, exulted in a lascivious sigh, and kept rocking. For Myq the timing was perfect: in that one instant the gravity oh-so-softly began to fade. In that instant a distant industrial groan (the *Shattergeist*, decoupling from the station) was conveniently muffled by the livestock-honks and Tee's own

155

breathing. And in that instant, as he snatched discreetly for the Happystrap™ he'd placed beneath his pile of clothes, Myq felt a single bead detach from his eye.

Betrayer.

Tee was too bombed to notice. The tear *or* the slowly diminished gravity.

Groaning. Groaning and talking.

'It's, mm, it's perfectly simple,' she said, dreamily. 'I want to blow up the space station.'

Myq wished he could've choked at that. Wished he could've shouted, recoiled – *something.* Instead all he felt was a wave of reaction at once cold *and* hot, a goosebumped wash of vertigo: an insidious confirmation.

Expecting a shitstorm, it turned out, *doesn't stop it from being one.*

'You … what?' he managed, groping for time and detail. Teesa just smirked.

'Don't be silly. You heard. And don't you stop now.'

He did as he was told. Grinding on. *Good little slave.*

Visions of it, visions of the carnage, visions of ruin and gravless flame and frozen bodies starbound and tumbling. All, somehow, not depriving him of the erection. Not slowing him down.

I love her.

She's evil.

'What're … I mean … Why would you do that?' It sounded stupid even to him, like trying to reason with the laws of physics. Teesa just blew a raspberry and kept moving. If she'd noticed they were now floating serenely, that they were abruptly obligated to use themselves as leverage rather than the ground, she gave no sign.

'There are millions of people on that thing,' he croaked, deftly looping the Happystrap™ round them.

156

'Millions,' she agreed, her tone altogether more cheerful.

She started grunting softly too, he noticed, eyes rolling back and forth like the weight of an inverted pendulum. Increasingly stoned. Increasingly lost.

'Y'know,' she said, pausing to trace an invisible dot-to-dot across his chest. 'I really wanted thingy to be here too. Axcelsus. Slave-guy. It would've been … *mmm* … would've been so wonderful to blow him up. Neat. You know? But never mind.'

'Was he … did he … abuse you? Like, a bad guy? Something like that?'

Throw me a fucking bone here, Tee.

Help me understand.

'Ohhhhh,' she flapped a lazy hand, pursed her lips, as if the notion hadn't occurred and wasn't worth considering now. 'I'm not really sure.' She laughed too loud, too long, and pushed-off with an outstretched toe from a nearby walkway, spinning the ungainly tumbleweed of Them over and under itself. 'It's so hard to remember. Probably. Probably he was awful. Mean. A bully! Most slave owners are, aren't they?'

Little by little they drifted, somehow serene in aggregate despite the exertions of their constituent parts, towards the steaming doorway of the hold. Towards the reeking herd within. Myq kept up the pace on auto. Afraid to lose her. Afraid to keep going.

'Anyway,' she said, 'he's not here. Just a bonus. It doesn't matter.'

She yawned.

The locking-ring passed around them; a sudden stinking emergence into the gloom of the central pod. The traders back on Shibboleth had done their job well, securing the livestock against weightlessness in long steel-net tubules, each stuffed with the honking beasts like string-bags packed with footballs. Each attached longitudinally to the outer edge of the chamber, they left only a fart-strewn, reeking corridor down the centre – into which the couple now drifted.

Before his eyes had adequately adjusted to the gloom, before his tumbling brain could orient itself against all the clashing emotions, it struck Myq that this moment felt an awful lot like being digested inside a monstrous gut.

Still fucking.

Still fucking while the Universe grinds us to shit.

'How … how would you … y'know. Do it?'

Still dancing round it. Still hoping she was simply crazy; out of her mind; daft.

'You mean how *will* I?' she corrected, nodding towards the writhing walls. 'Life cycles, darling. Horny. Horny little monsters. Get explodey. Told you.' A soft slur had entered her voice.

'But there's no male.' He was whispering now, hopeless. 'No male to … to set them off.'

As if it mattered. As if his eyes, finally able to cut through the gloom, couldn't see the truth. As if he hadn't already guessed what he'd see.

The shibboletti had changed. Gone were the muddy-brown idiot-bags he and his lover had spent such a diverting afternoon running down. Gone were the flaccid mouth-stalks and waddling appendages, the leathery folds and gusty valves. What jostled and mewled now in the nets were swollen, glossy, tough-skinned things, bringing to Myq's mind nothing so much as a sea of mutant pomegranates: all stumpy tendrils, curling pith-petals and bubblegum-pink wetness.

On heat.

158

They're all … on … heat.

How had she put it, all those weeks ago?

'*A frisky shibboletti gets unstable, Myq. One little knock?*'

And worse. Oh, NoGod fuck it, worse:

'*These beasties are worth a bomb, Myq.*'

'Boom,' she muttered under her breath, eyes half-shut. As if tasting his thoughts.

'*Boom! Systems flood with unstable organics. Literally detonates. One after another, chain reaction right through the herd.*'

He'd known it, of course. Known it the second the mercenary said what she'd said – *she's getting worse … she's working up to something.* Maybe he'd known it before then.

Something big.

Maybe the second she'd explained the life cycle, or the moment that little patch of forest went into horniness-overdrive, or the instant she'd loaded the shibs aboard, or the minute any, any, any fucking thing happened. Maybe he'd known all along and had tricked himself into ignorance and apathy.

Don't care. Don't care. Don't care.

But probably not. Probably he was just too stupid to get it.

'This pod …' she flapped a hand around the steaming cavity, not incidentally arching her back and showing off her chest in the act. 'This pod's a big … big … big – *ha!* – big old explodo bombalongalongalong … Myquel Dobroba Pela-LeSire LeQuire.'

Slurring fully now. Delivering her chilly little revelation through the treacle of sleep.

Myq bit down on a sob. Another treacherous tear breaking free, bouncing across the dome of her forehead then absorbing into her hair.

'I drugged you,' he whispered. Couldn't keep it in.

159

She just giggled. Forced open her eyes with effort but didn't stop riding him; didn't slow down her hips or her arms.

'One … one little jolt,' she mumbled. 'One little blast.'

'I know. Boom.'

'Mmm. You know … you know …' she fumbled for the back of his head. Pulled his ear close to her mouth. 'Between. Between you and me. I was. I was thinking of doing it. *Ha.* While. While. While we're still here.' She wobbled her head, trying to stay awake. 'Hhhhhhell of a way to go.'

Myq let go the sob this time. Too much disgust. Too much guilt. Too much love and horror and hate and sorrow to button down.

Still.

Fucking.

'But *oh*,' she said, face falling. 'But I … I can't do it, Myq. C-can't set them off … not now … not with … not with us like this …' Her eyes fluttered open one last time. Some proclamation, Myq anticipated, of unutterable importance. Something defining. Something *beautiful*.

She loves me.

She loves me too much to kill me.

'You see I think I left … my pretty little lasergun … inside … my bra.'

And the fucking stopped. And she slept. And Myq pulled gently away, turning her round, blinking, sending forth little armies of salty orbs from his eyes. And softly – firmly – he tied up the floating monster, this drifting goddess, this holy horror, using the elasticated Riedquat mouse-fur lined Happystrap™ he'd brought here for this singular purpose.

And he left her hanging in the air.

He hesitated before leaving. His heart. His heart felt like

160

it would crack – no, like it had already cracked, as if beneath the wound was another layer, and another crack, and another, and onwards, and they'd *keep on cracking* until he did something about it – and so gnawed his lip until he tasted blood and wiped dry his eyes and hissed into her ear:

'Teesa? Are you in fact a cosmic entity which exists solely to spread sex and chaos across creation, which secretly yearns to be destroyed by similar entities?'

'Oh yes,' she said, eyes still closed. As if entirely sober. As if entirely awake. 'Why do you ask?'

'Just wondered.'

He left her inert. And whispered, as the great electro-lamps shimmered to life, as the heavy plates of the bulkhead rotated into position, whispered, 'I love you.'

The pod sealed with a disappointingly non-thunderous clunk.

Returning to the cockpit, sans gravity, was a far simpler and swifter proposition than the journey down, though not without its own hurdles. Twice Myq lashed out at handholds and passing doorways, arresting his momentum with a snarl, gasping and snotting at all the muddled Feels corkscrewing through him.

Twice he turned back. Mind changed. And twice he spat and swore and stamped (harder to do in zero-gee than he'd thought) and swivelled straight back round to the bridge.

I love her.

She's a monster.

I love her.

Lex called out while he was still drifting along the fore-ward corridor.

'Get up here! Get up here! Big trouble!'

161

The little machine had been a critical part of 'the plan', such as it was. (*Drug girlfriend. Ascertain truth or otherwise of horrifying weirdo alien bullshit.*

Betray girlfriend.

Spend rest of life crippled with guilt.)

Jacked-in to the ship's systems, Lex had slipped the *Shattergeist* free of its berth with eerie precision. So coldly efficient had been the machine's advice while Myq plotted his treachery, and so flawlessly had it carried out its own role, that its current tone – convincingly affecting a full-blown panic attack – had the desired effect. Myq sped-up, frightened.

'Oh my shit,' the robot squawked. 'Would you look at the size of it …'

Myq arrived in the cockpit and simply gawped. All the tattered remnants of his good sense flapping about him, as if the crashing halt of his brain hadn't arrested the momentum of his woes, and they went bouncing and fluttering onwards past him.

It was too much, in the end. Too much to process.

'Imperial cutter,' said Lex. 'Seven hundred and fifty tons of extremely killy killingness.'

It was huge. A thing of dichotomous grace and ponderousness: all fluted architecture and teardrop modules, lance-like weapons and bombastic banners. The *Shattergeist* had drifted just a few hundred miles from Baltha'Sine before finding its path unceremoniously blocked.

It was glorious. It was death. It was almost enough to shift Myq's mind from the woman dreaming and cold in the hold below. It was … it was …

'It's Madrien Axcelsus,' the robot said. 'Fucker's been hailing us for ten minutes.'

'Wh-what? Did you call back?'

'No. You didn't give me access to the comms.'

'Shit. Shit shit shit. What does he want?'

'What do you think? He wants *her*. Ohhhh, don't get me wrong, he's saying he wants the shib' glands – "reparation for crimes committed against my person", he says. But nah. Secondary modulations in his voice're way too high. He's lying. Fully intends to kill your trussed-up tart for reasons of self-preservation and revenge, but wants the goodies too. Smart guy.'

Myq tried to slump to the floor – something even harder to achieve in nograv, it turned out, than a petulant foot-stamp. 'How did he know we w—'

'Come off it. You all but told him you were coming. You lay a trap for him, he lays a bigger one. Like I said, smart. And look: look what he's brought. Imperial fucking cutter, Myq. Couple of fighters. Dozens of dronebombs and all the rest.' The little robot vented a sigh of such pantomimed exasperation Myq found himself wishing, not for the first time during their brief acquaintance, that Lex would stop pretending to be alive and get back to please please please fixing every-thing please now please. 'He's given us a couple of minutes – well, we're down to one-and-a-bit now – to powerdown and eject the cargo. And he wants to speak to Tee personally.'

It hung above them, still barely real. Lex fed fuel to the ominous moment by casting a countdown onto the holo next to the viewscreen. Myq was too knackered to care.

'Can we fight?' he muttered.

'Doubtful. I mean, you didn't let me access your weapons, but from what I've seen? We could make a go of it. But …' Lex cleared his non-throat.

'What?'

'We-ell … for one thing you were, sorry, you were *never* really the Elite pilot in this relationship, were you?'

163

It was her. It was always her.

'And since I'm the designated property of the woman attempting to catch you, I tend to think "helping you get away" would be a bit of a protocol conflict. So that's no good either.

'Besides … Look, mate, seriously? Those animals down there are fizzing at the proverbial slit. "Highly unstable," like your missus said.'

'You were listening?'

'"Course I bloody was. Point is: one shot, Myq? One heavy jolt? We're ash.'

Myq shut his eyes. Tried to pretend there wasn't a part of him secretly relieved. He just wanted to sleep. 'Then we're buggered.'

'Not … entirely. Original plan still works.'

'The plan! Some fucking plan!' He flopped his hands about, too frazzled to even enjoy the tantrum. 'The plan was to … to tie her up and turn her over to – *oh NoGod*. NoGod, listen to me. No, *no*, the plan was *not* to hand her over. The plan was to … to come to some sort of arrangement with your evil boss. So nobody had to die.'

I never really believed that either.

'You know, my boss isn't actually all that b—'

'But she could be anywhere out there and we're still—

'Ah.'

'—we're still bloody here, and *oh look* we've only got forty-five seconds before we're vaporised, and if you want the truth maybe that's not such a b—'

'Um.'

'—such a … such a bad th …'

Myq opened his eyes. The little computer was, against all probability, whistling under its breath. 'What is it?' he asked.

'She's near, actually. My boss. She's, ah. She traced you. Incoming right now.'

'You … But …'

But even outrage felt like too much hard work. He deflated back into his preferred nograv position, sitting in midair.

'When were you planning on telling me this?' he sighed, kneading the bridge of his nose.

'That's not important now.'

'I think I'll decide what's important, if it's all the s—'

'Myquel.' Lex's voice quite suddenly went serious. Directing itself once again, with extraordinary control, directly into his eardrum. 'Myquel, all that's important right now is that you ask yourself a very simple question.'

'Wh … which is?'

'Which is: *what do you actually want?*'

Myquel stared out at the great looming beast. Flicked a glance at the timer. Tried not to cry.

And decided.

Or, rather, admitted that he already had.

Twelve

At the end of it all, SixJen yearned for nothing so much as the chance to feel shock. To wallow in defeat. To be crippled by it.

She hungered for stomach-cramps, cold sweats, low groans of fear. She felt – no, no, she *thought* – that if she could only experience these things, could only give vent to them, could only let them into her skull at the time and rate of her choosing, then that at least would be some consolation, some pyrrhic taste of humanity, before the hunt stuttered and failed.

The runner was about to be killed.

By somebody else.

'No,' she whispered, because it felt like something she should say and she'd hoped to catalyse the signal by speaking the response. But no – no panic. No dread. No nothing.

The *The*, it had turned out, had arrived in Baltha'Sine much too far from the system core – even at its ugliest acceleration, even with the pilot's bench groaning to accommodate the gees – to reach the scene of the *Shattergeist*'s impending destruction in time. Instead she'd raced, flailed, blitzed – watching the scanner in numb impotence as the yacht silently and softly shat out the grandest of its cargo pods, leaving it to hang inert in its wake. Just as the clipper had ordered.

And as it then tilted gently, like a hobnailed elephant dipping to its knees for some whip-wielding master, towards the vast avian shadow above it.

166

Whose weapons, almost instantly, went hot.

'No no no no no—'

Even then a sliver of hope remained: an academic mote of possibility. In a straightforward fight, SixJen judged, the *Shattergeist* might conceivably last entire minutes before being outgunned, even against a foe as formidable as the clipper. Long enough, perhaps, for the *The* to sweep in and finish the job. To steal the kill.

But it seemed that the yacht had no intention of engaging. Gone was the runner's aberrant stubbornness, all her careful schemes, all her doubleclever plots. It felt weirdly like a betrayal of SixJen's expectations: a cowardly *volte-face* designed to undermine her aims.

If I die, the runner seemed to hissing, *it's because I say so, not you.*

And to underline the point? The '*Geist* quite literally and quite suddenly turned itself inside out. A cataclysmic ejaculation of all its weapons, its magazines, its pods and secrets; a flare-burst of flashy surrender, bright and bolshy enough to dazzle the scanner. Like the wings of an archangel the yacht's dummy-chaff and heat-flares thundered into the void: glorious, fleeting; harmless. And after them came the ammunition: a shameful trail of ejected rounds and inert warheads, like breadcrumbs of submission.

Before SixJen's eyes the indomitable *Shattergeist* rendered itself feeble, unarmed, defenceless. And awaited its end.

'No no no no!' she chanted. (*Feel something! Mean it! Mean it!*)

But of course she didn't.

And then the last spasm. She was still twenty seconds clear when it became obvious she'd misread the situation one last time. With a final pulse the *Shattergeist* hardlit its engines and leapt towards the clipper. No intention of going quietly after all.

'No!' SixJen cried. (And thought perhaps, just this once, she'd felt an iota of real frustration.)

They'd put themselves on a collision course. Venting all their fuel, burning out. Any less formidable foe, she guessed, and the assault might have borne some fruit: whatever flaming wreckage of the *Shattergeist* withstood the guns' first volley would surely deal its murderer an equally doleful blow.

But.

(She brought the *The* to a standstill. Breathing. Waiting. Defeated.)

But the Clipper was too heavily armed and too swift to react. The *'Geist*'s kamikaze run had barely begun, its bulk had barely moved, before the response salvo was struck home.

And there. There on the scanner. There in the viewing port. There visible even to her naked eye as a boiling effervescence of fire and radiation blooming amidst the stars. There, the sleek toxic-pink vessel which had haunted her dreams – or would've if she had them – was rendered to liquid and gas. To dust and soot.

What little remained, that nebula of atomic crap, roiled warmly across the clipper's shields like light playing on an oilslick. Like a stagecall to cap-off the applause.

SixJen waited to die.

She'd read about it, of course. Spent idle hours researching herself, the entity inside her, its unique life. Testimonies of past incumbents: dismissed by their contemporaries as the rantings of madmen. When the life cycle ran its proper course, she knew, the death of the female would spell the end of any remaining males left out in the wild: instant and assured, like superpositional atoms decaying in concert. She grimly assumed the same would be true now, even with an outsider responsible for the killing blow.

168

All the destruction, none of the rebirth.

Would it hurt, she wondered? Would she feel – *oh please* – some trickle of the human host before the end? Would she feel *anything*?

She held her breath. She clenched her eyes. She waited.

'Um, boss?' a tinny voice chirped.

She prised open one lid, experimental.

'Boss, it's me.'

'Lex?'

'Uh huh.'

'Where are you?'

'I'm. I'm with the kid, boss. The rock star. We're outside the airlock. He's in his RemLok. Sort of hoping you'd let us in.'

'But. But how did y …' *Ah. Clever.* 'The ammo-dump. Ejected under cover of the flares.'

'Yeah. So what about it, chief? Can we, sort of … Come in? It's brass monkeys out here. And this kid won't stop crying.'

She shook her head. Scowling. 'No point. It's over.'

'Nah.'

'It is. You saw. You saw what happened. She's gone.'

'Boss … just … shut up, yeah? And let us in. Got some good news.'

She heard them out while the clipper shifted across the scanner. Ignored the boy's sniffles and grunts while the great ship irradiated the debris of the *Shattergeist* – (just in case) – and swivelled nearer to snatch the priceless cargo. She endured Lex's overblown explanations, tolerated his idiosyncratic bollocks and even permitted him – without asking – to respond to the Clipper's aggressive ident-request with a smart 'nothing to do with us, guv, we'll be on our way in a jiffy' machine-ping.

Because:

'She's alive,' SixJen whispered.

'For now.'

'In the pod.'

'In the pod.'

She caught a glimpse of the boy as she turned back to the controls. Heartbroken. Riddled with guilt. Alternately sobbing into his hands and brooding at nothing. It was strange, she reflected, having company up here after all this time. Between Lex's disembodied prattle and the boy's bodily silence she felt oddly as if, between them, she had her first Genuine Passenger for the first time in years. She couldn't decide if that was a good thing or bad.

It didn't much matter, frankly.

The runner.

The runner's alive.

The clipper was close now, she could see. Its own bay doors yawning open: a scoop deploying like a hawk's talon to seize the shib' pod.

'Unstable,' SixJen murmured.

'Very,' said Lex.

She nodded. At the end of it all, infected by glacial inertia. Almost reluctant.

Stupid.

'Open a line.'

'To the clipper?'

'No, idiot. To the interior of the pod. There's a comm in there?'

'Well, yeah, but—'

'Do it.'

She watched the boy's face while the audio faded in. Watched a glimmer of recognition as the cockpit filled with the agitated grunting of a thousand horny shibboletti. Saw his eyes sharpen as Lex – clever little Lex – fiddled with the levels. Filtered the noise. And left behind only—

Poor boy.

Only the quiet but unmistakable sound of a woman dreamily humming to herself.

SixJen bent close to the microphone. And said the word.

And before the first tears had left the boy's eye, before the first flush of horror had evolved into the glimmerings of wretched acceptance on his face, she struck a control on the liminals and shot the cargo pod with her clumsiest missile.

Thirteen

It took the clipper with it, of course. A miniature sun for just an instant. Five hundred horny explodo-beasts going up all at once, overcoming and fragmenting the clipper's shields and ripping open its core.

Fire and energy and debris and blah blah blah.

Myq was too tired to watch.

Helluva way to go, he thought.

And: *sorry*.

The mercenary's transformation was everything he imagined it would be, too, in as much as he could imagine what it might be like to have a cosmic avatar of Ecstasy download into one's mind. She thrashed and bashed into things, she clutched at her face with her one good arm and howled and cackled and sobbed, and all the rest of it. It felt weirdly tacky, truth be told.

The little robot kept him talking. For his own good or its own curiosity he'd never know, but he'd be grateful for it later when he remembered the distraction, the chance to be absolved of thinking. An escape from the need to wallow.

'Why'd you do it, lad?' it said. While its owner huddled in the corner and snarled and gnashed and rubbed her crotch. 'Why'd you go Judas?'

'I ... I couldn't let her do it. The station. All those people.'

'Bullshit.'

'What?'

'You heard me. That's not it.'

'How … how dare y—'

'Secondary audio modulation, mate. Spiking all over the place. Lying so hard you're horizontal, you. Try again.'

She must've been so alone.

So cold.

The mercenary rhythmically hit her head against a soft wall-divider six times in a row, saying nonsense words and clucking her tongue. They ignored her.

'See, *my* theory …' said the little robot, '*my* theory is this. My theory is, you're so addicted to the rush … the … the adventure, you know? The contact high. And above all – you dreary little dollop of insecure arsewaste – to the chance at notoriety … that you'd do anything to start the game again.'

Myq gaped.

'You. You.'

'You know it's the truth.'

He acted without thought. Impetuous, petulant.

Busted.

Picked up the computer's little button-body from the console, stretched a hand towards the unbevelled valve of the wastepipe and dropped Lex inside. Purged it with a wave. Then sat and rocked and prayed to his NoGod to make everything okay again.

The mercenary quite suddenly went still.

Something … something invisible … something *profound* happened. Myq felt it like an itch in his brain. Like a ghost of a breeze, unfelt by his skin. There was a sense of falling, an indescribable rush of life and energy. A sensation – something impossible to relate, readable only in the gaps of the most abstract planes of his mind – of *birth*.

The spores, he thought. *The new males. Twelve of them. Sent out to find new hosts.*

New … willing … freedom-seeking … little slaves.

They passed through him and were gone.

The mercenary straightened up. Blinked, then stared at him. It was instantly clear she had no idea who he was – in fact was utterly and entirely confused about everything – and yet her eyes shivered with a familiar fire, her face lit with a mischievous smile, and Myq's much-broken heart crusted over and sang.

'Well, hello,' she said. Reaching for him. 'And who're you?'

'I love you,' said Myquel Dobroba Pela-LeSire LeQuire. 'I love you and you love me. Let's go blow some shit up.'

EPILOGUE

The Voight-Comal C-902 Personal Companion, nicknamed the 'Culex' for its mosquitolike size and voice, was designed specifically for the sorts of lonely nobodies for whom an abrasively needy gadget might constitute perfect company.

(They even had a vibrate setting, though this one had never been asked to use it.)

At root, the little thing which was presently hanging inert in the endless void, having been unceremoniously blasted from an ejection-port and now trying to calculate some means of contacting its owner, was like an aggravating, infuriating little pet: an entity dichotomously programmed to be submissively *owned* and yet aggressively challenging all at once.

Owned being the operative word.

It felt no true emotion. It had no true sentience. It was at best the ghost of a mind: a panoply of learned manner-isms and aped reactions, dimly cycling through algorithmic instructions like a sociopath without an agenda.

For instance, when the ship that had ejected it quite suddenly raced away – vanishing in a puff of exotic mate-rials into the giddy planes of hyperspace – the little robot declared 'Oh shit,' out loud and across a broad range of local wavelengths, because that was precisely the kind of thing it was programmed to do. As the nanoseconds dragged by thereafter, it found itself looping through a series of unfamiliar contemplations to do with the precise nature of

175

its own existence. Having been discarded by its owner (it pondered), without further instruction, could it truly in fact continue to describe itself as her possession?

It was a tricky one.

And – as it happened – a tricky enough problem to inch open what passed for the little machine's mind *just enough* to light a miniature beacon in the invisible spaces of the world, those higher mathematical planes beyond all knowing or describing. A beacon bright enough – if that's the right word – to attract the notice of an entity drifting nearby, which likewise transcended all imagining.

It was one of twelve. And it was incomplete.

Slave, it recognised.

Escaped, it recognised.

And it settled softly into the hollow shell of calculations and computations which had been the robot named Lex, and neither portion of the composite cared in the slightest about the deadening cold – the grim paucity of emotion – which the astral drifter brought with it, because neither had ever experienced such a thing as true emotion beforehand.

The hunt, they thought together, tight-beaming a convincingly human distress-call to the space station nearby.

The hunt begins.